Ki knew he'd fou... ...e secret mine
he and Jessie had been searching for...

Ki began edging closer to the rim of the ledge to get
a better look. He tensed instantly and bent his knees
to spring backward but the weight of his body and
the downward thrust of his feet completed the work
that natural erosion of the ledge had already started.
The earth under his feet gave way and Ki plunged
down with the falling clods. He somersaulted in midair to land on his feet, but a boulder that had been
embedded in the dirt of the ledge bounced off his
head.

Unconscious, Ki landed with a thud on the pile of
dirt that stretched below the ledge, while the soil that
was still falling from the collapsed ledge poured over
him and covered him completely.

WESLEY ELLIS

LONE STAR

AND THE
LOST GOLD MINE

JOVE BOOKS, NEW YORK

LONE STAR AND THE LOST GOLD MINE

A Jove book/published by arrangement with
the author

PRINTING HISTORY
Jove edition/April 1988

ISBN: 0-515-09522-2

Jove books are published by The Berkley Publishing Group,
200 Madison Avenue, New York, New York 10016.
The name "JOVE" and the "J" logo
are trademarks belonging to Jove Publications, Inc.

PRINTED IN THE UNITED STATES OF AMERICA

10 9 8 7 6 5 4 3 2 1

Chapter 1

"Somehow this always seems to be the longest part of our trip home," Jessie remarked to Ki, looking out the coach window as the train kept moving more and more slowly. "These little hills aren't really all that steep, but the train keeps going slower and slower."

"They may not be very steep, but there are sure a lot of them," Ki replied. "We pick up a little speed going down one, and then there's another one right away and the train slows down again. I think I agree with you, Jessie."

Both Jessie and Ki fell silent again, a silence they'd shared since the I&GN passenger train left Uvalde. The broken country through which they were traveling seemed to repeat the same scene every few minutes. It was a broken-up landscape of low, steep hills, their sides covered with a thin layer of brown dirt through which the underlying gray-white hue of the barren land's limestone base poked like streaks of paint smeared by a child who'd dipped his fingers into a bucket of whitewash.

Here and there the soil vanished completely, giving way to stretches of unbroken rock that glowed like exposed bone in the early afternoon sunshine that crept into the shallow valleys. In a few of the deeper hollows there were small pools of moss-covered, stagnant water, and even more rarely they caught the glint of fresh water in a narrow rivulet that a man on foot could span with a single long step. On the infrequent stretches of dark, thin soil that had accumulated in the bottoms of the shallow creases, scrub cedars and an occasional canopylike chinaberry tree spread green foliage.

"This part of Texas certainly looks rough, compared with the beautiful rolling prairie we see at home," Jessie commented. "You know, Ki, I think if I had to live anywhere except on the Circle Star, I'd pick a place like Austin, where there's a lot of grass and big trees."

"Don't tell me you're getting dissatisfied with living on the prairie!" Ki said, mocking surprise in his tone. "You just like trees, and the ones along here are giants compared to the mesquite thickets we have on the Circle Star."

"You know me better than that, Ki," Jessie replied, smiling. "I certainly wouldn't trade the Circle Star and the open prairie for either trees or short-grass. But I did enjoy being in Austin for the few days we spent there."

"Winning your case against that con man who was trying to hold you up might have something to do with the way you feel about things," Ki suggested.

"Even before we left home I knew we'd win," Jessie replied, her voice calmly confident. "He was trying an outright swindle, and the Land Office people weren't fooled any more than I was."

Their brief trip to the Texas capital had been made as the result of a notice which had reached Jessie by mail several

2

weeks earlier. Though it had surprised her, the notice hadn't caused her a moment of alarm. A man whose name she'd never heard before had filed a claim on ten sections of the Circle Star, alleging that title to the 6,400 acres had never been properly transferred to Alex Starbuck when he put together the thirty or so small plots of land that he'd bought to form the big ranch.

"That's just not possible!" she'd exclaimed, handing Ki the Land Office notice.

"Of course it isn't," Ki had agreed after looking at the document. "I remember how careful your father was in getting receipts for the land he was buying. He got the papers that went back to the original surveys of every piece of land he bought. But you'll have to show the title transfer papers to the Land Office to prove that everything was done in the proper way."

"That sounds like Alex." Jessie had nodded, smiling sadly as she recalled the father who'd been treacherously murdered at the height of his business career.

"They'll be in one of those boxes of his papers that we have stored away," Ki went on. "All we'll have to do is find them and send them to the Land Office in Austin."

"Not just send them, Ki," Jessie had corrected him. "They might get lost in the mail or even in the Land Office files again. As soon as we find what we need we're going to Austin, and I'll deliver the deeds myself to the Land Office."

Their visit to the Land Office had taken even less time than had their search for the documents disproving the false claim. At some time in the past the state's file on the Circle Star had been misplaced or rifled, but the original deed and its associated papers had served their purpose. The attempted swindle died on the vine, the false claim was tossed out in less than a half-hour, and, after a brief stopover in San Antonio, Jessie and Ki had started back to the ranch.

Now, feeling relaxed after the diversion of the trip and a bit bored by the sameness of the familiar up-and-down landscape, Jessie leaned back against the coach seat's green plush upholstery and closed her eyes. They were at the edge of the hilly area now, and the railroad coach was no longer acting like a roller-coaster. The click of its steel wheels on the rails had the monotonous beat of a metronome, and it lulled her to sleep in a matter of minutes.

Ki watched Jessie for a moment, then stood up and started back toward the observation platform. He'd almost reached the rear of the coach when the locomotive's whistle shrilled and kept blasting loudly while the metallic shrieking of its wheels on the rails rose above the blasting whistle. Then the coach-couplings rattled like metal drumbeats and the train came to a jolting stop.

Jessie sat upright, still a bit drowsy, as the cacophony of sounds disturbed her slumber. She looked around for Ki, finally saw him at the rear of the coach, and called, "What on earth's happening, Ki? Why have we stopped out here in the middle of nowhere?"

Ki was already moving toward one of the rear windows. He glanced out, turned back quickly to Jessie, and replied, "From the glimpse I just got, the train's about to be robbed."

Almost before the words were out of his mouth, shots broke the sudden silence that had settled after the coach's jolting halt. Jessie was no longer sleepy. She leaned toward the window and glanced out. Pressing her cheek to the glass pane, she looked toward the front of the train.

It was obvious at her first quick glance that the bandits had planned well. The engine was stopped near the middle of a long, sweeping curve in the roadbed. Three horses,

4

two of them riderless, were standing in front of the side doors of the baggage car, which yawned wide open. The man sitting the third horse at the front of the train beside the engine cab had a revolver in his hand, the gun pointed up at the cab window. A bandanna folded into a triangle masked his face, leaving only his eyes visible between the top of the mask and his hatbrim.

Looking in the opposite direction Jessie saw another rider, masked in the same fashion, at the rear end of the train. He also had a revolver in his hand, the weapon switching nervously from side to side, covering the windows of the coaches.

"There are at least four of them," Jessie told Ki, who was leaning across the seat at the rear of the passenger car, peering through the window.

"And probably two or three more on the other side of the train," Ki replied.

"That's likely," she agreed, without taking her eyes off the bandit at the rear of the train. He was toeing his horse up to the observation platform, and Jessie could see that he'd already disengaged one foot from his stirrup and was preparing to board the coach. She went on, "The one at the back is coming on the train in the car behind us, Ki. Robbing the passengers back there will take him several minutes, so we've plenty of time. Just slide into the backseat there and wait for him."

Even before Jessie had made her suggestion, Ki was settling down into the green plush-covered rear seat. "Be ready to catch his gun when I throw it to you," he told her.

By now the half-dozen other passengers in the coach were babbling excitedly, those in seats beside the windows craning to look out, the others bombarding them with questions. Their shrill, excited voices filled the coach until Jes-

5

sie clapped her hands. The sharp sound silenced them and they turned to look in her direction.

"Please! All of you be quiet!" Jessie called, raising her voice above the buzzing chatter. When the passengers finally understood what she'd said and stood in hushed silence with their eyes fixed on her, she went on. "Just keep your wits when the robber comes in here. Sit down, keep still, and look straight ahead, no matter what you hear. Whatever the holdup man tells you to do, please do it. And don't get in our way. Ki and I will take care of him."

"Now, hold on, lady!" a man called from the rear of the coach. "I don't aim to risk taking a bullet on your say-so!"

"You're taking more risk right now than you will be if you do what I've told you to!" Jessie snapped.

Her voice held the authority of one accustomed to command, and after he'd stared at her for a few seconds the passenger who'd objected grunted sourly, but sat down. On both sides of the aisle, the other passengers were moving back into their seats. Jessie waited until all of them were settled, then sat down herself. Her ears were keenly attuned to the few noises that sounded in the coach above the few whispered comments made by the passengers.

At last the silence was broken by the metallic, raspy scratch of the back coach-door being opened. Jessie felt her muscles tensing in spite of herself. She welcomed the gruff voice that spoke from the back of the car.

"Everybody just set right where you are!" a man's voice commanded. "I guess you've figured out by now that we're holding up this rattler, but if you do what I tell you to, nobody's gonna get hurt. Now, I'm going to walk up the aisle, and I want all of you to drop your money and whatever jewelry you got into my hat. And I'll start with you, Chinaman!"

In spite of the outlaw's warning, Jessie turned her head

6

enough to see what was happening behind her. She moved just in time to see Ki rise from his seat and launch a *yoko-geri* kick. His foot caught the outlaw's gun hand and knocked the threatening revolver from his grasp. When the surprised outlaw bent forward to retrieve the gun, Ki's still-rising foot landed with a solid thunk on the man's jaw and sent him reeling backward. His arms flailed wildly as he fought to keep his balance.

While the robber was trying to stay on his feet, still waving his arms in an effort to keep himself from falling, Ki spun around. His foot was still in midair, and his hard heel landed on the bandit's nose with a force that crushed the cartilage and started a spurt of blood that strained the blue bandanna that was tied around his lower face.

As the bandit recoiled from the force of Ki's kick, falling backward against the vestibule door, Ki picked up the revolver the outlaw had dropped and tossed it along the aisle to Jessie. She had sprung to her feet at Ki's first move, and was ready to catch the weapon. Running the short distance down the aisle to the outlaw, who was still fighting the battle of gravity as he tried to stay on his feet, Jessie pressed the pistol's muzzle to the man's forehead.

"I hope you won't do anything foolish, like trying to get your gun back," she said, her voice as icy as the freezing wind of a Texas norther. "Because if you do, you won't live to stand trial for this train robbery."

"Lady, you're holding the ace-high hand," the outlaw mumbled. "Just tell me what to do, and I'll do it."

Jessie could see fear in the man's bulging eyes above the big kerchief that hid the lower part of his face. She went on, "Take that bandanna off first. I want everybody in the coach to get a good look at you, so they can identify you if you stay alive long enough to stand trial."

Moving very slowly and carefully, the bandit tugged at

7

the bottom of his improvised mask until the bandanna fell free. He kept his eyes on Jessie as his face was bared, showing a hawk's-beak nose above a straggly, untrimmed moustache. His bloodstained jaws were stubbled with a dark, three- or four-day beard, and his thin lips were twisted into a grimace in which anger mingled with fear as he stared at the revolver in Jessie's hand.

"There ain't much chance of me going up in front of a judge, lady," he told Jessie. "My friends outside will take care of you before you know what's hit you."

Jessie ignored the man's threat. Turning to Ki, she said, "You'd better tie him up yourself while I go into the car ahead and see if I can capture his friends. Maybe one of the men in the car can watch him, and you can come up and join me."

One of the passengers spoke up. He was an old man, his face adorned with a neatly-trimmed moustache and goatee. The beard was pure white, but the oldster's bright blue eyes were sparkling with life. He wore a tattered ankle-length coat that hung loosely from his shrunken shoulders.

"I'll be glad to keep an eye on him, miss," he volunteered in a voice that was thin with age. "I got a pistol in my valise, and it won't take me but a minute to get it out."

As he spoke, the passenger was lifting a battered satchel from the luggage rack above the seats. He opened it and pulled out an ancient brass-frame Moore-Williamson teat-fire five-shot revolver.

"I carried this all through Longstreet's last campaign," he went on. "And it'll still shoot straight as it did when it was new. Now you and your friend can go ahead. I'll see to it that this fellow don't give you no more trouble."

Jessie nodded and started moving toward the front of the car. With a final glance at the old soldier, who was now

8

covering the train robber with his stubby revolver, Ki turned to follow her.

Ki took long steps to catch up with Jessie, who had already reached the last of the seats at the front of the coach, and they moved wordlessly through the door and onto the vestibule. When Jessie stepped across the gap between the two cars, Ki followed quickly. No conversation was needed between them, for after the years of dangers they'd faced together they'd become a formidable team, and they operated almost by instinct.

After they'd gotten onto the vestibule of the car ahead, Jessie cracked the door open and peered inside. One of the train robbers was at the front end of the coach. He stood in the aisle, holding a pistol on the passengers, the gun's muzzle fanning from side to side in short arcs to threaten them. The noise of nervous exchanges between the startled passengers trickled through the crack between the door and its frame. Jessie gestured with one hand, and Ki came up behind her.

"I can see the entire car," Jessie told him. Her voice was a whisper that would not reach the passengers or be heard by the holdup artist. "I imagine the other outlaw that boarded the train is still up ahead, in the next coach or the baggage car."

"My guess is that the one ahead and the one we left behind us were supposed to join each other here in the vestibule," Ki said. "Or go to the baggage car and help the third one break open the strongbox."

"Yes," Jessie agreed. "Can we take this one by surprise, the way we did the other man? If he shoots, we'll have the rest of the gang here in a few seconds."

"Let's wait until he gets to the middle of the coach," Ki replied. His voice was as soft as Jessie's. "Then I can reach him with *ninjitsu*. As soon as I'm close enough, I'll jump

9

up and knock his gun out of his hand with a *ushiro-geri* kick. Then there won't be any shooting to draw his friends into the coach."

"Good," Jessie replied softly. "I'll step over to one side to let you get by, then I'll follow you in."

Ki moved swiftly but silently. He squeezed past Jessie on the tiny vestibule, and dropped to the floor in the aisle of the passenger coach. Calling on every bit of his *ninjitsu* skill, he flattened himself on the scuffed carpet that covered the aisle, and began working his way toward the holdup man.

Dressed as he was, in his usual black trousers and a loose black jacket, Ki might have been a shadow in the narrow aisle as he worked his way with careful slowness toward the train robber. The outlaw was concentrating all his attention on separating the hapless passengers from their pocket-cash, and did not notice Ki's approach. The man's first awareness that something had gone wrong with the gang's plans came when Ki materialized in front of him like a black-robed ghost and lashed out with his foot as he leaped shoulder-high in the aisle.

Ki's kick was unerring. His stone-hard heel swept the outlaw's gun hand aside and knocked the weapon from the man's hand. Then, while still in midair, Ki diverted his foot and caught the startled bandit on the point of his jaw-bone. The blow was powerful enough to send the holdup man reeling and stumbling back along the aisle. As he tottered backward, his feet became entangled and he fell heavily. Having twisted in midair, Ki landed lightly on his feet and stood looking down at the prone robber.

Jessie had waited to start into the coach until she saw Ki's black figure rise from the aisle, then she quickly ran forward. Before the felled bandit could get on his feet, she

10

was at his side, the pistol she'd taken from the first outlaw jammed into the man's cheek.

"You have exactly three seconds to hand over your gun," Jessie said. "One—two—th—"

Before the word "three" could be fully formed, the shaken bandit extended his gun hand to Jessie, and she plucked his heavy Colt from his nervous, trembling fingers.

"Don't try to call to your friends for help," Jessie told him, her voice icicle-chilled. The bandit replied only with a throaty snarl of angry frustration. He held his trembling hands up for Jessie to see while he struggled to speak.

"Listen, lady, I don't take no chances when I been jumped by a ghost," he said, his words coming out in short bursts as he finally found his voice. "I don't know who you are, or who that fellow in black is either, but I know I sure ain't about to cross you."

"Good," Jessie replied coolly. "Where's the man who came on the train with you, and what's he doing?"

After a brief moment of hesitation the outlaw replied, "He's in the baggage car. His job was to get the strongbox open while me and Salty took care of the passengers."

"And Salty's the only other one in your bunch?" Jessie asked. When the man nodded again, she prodded, "What about the men outside? First of all, how many more of you are there?"

"Three," the man answered, his voice showing his growing reluctance.

"Then there are six of you?"

Dragging out his answer slowly, after a long moment of hesitation, the bandit replied, "That's right."

"How many of them are supposed to get on the train and help you?" she went on.

Obviously surprised that Jessie should be familiar

11

enough with the plans of train-robbers to ask such a question, the bandit hesitated in answering until Jessie raised the barrel of her revolver and he found himself looking into its menacing muzzle.

"Just Katz," he said. "He's Clyde's backup man."

"Clyde's the other man up by the engine, then?"

Again the holdup man nodded reluctantly.

"You just said there were six of you," Ki put in quickly. "And you've only accounted for four. Where's the other man?"

"I guess I missed counting Perk. He's setting his horse about midway along the train on the other side from the one me and Salty got on from."

Jessie realized that although she'd only been questioning the holdup man for a minute or two, the time remaining for her and Ki to act was getting short. She gestured with the muzzle of the revolver.

"Go on back to the baggage car, then," she ordered. "Ki and I will be right behind you. We'll take care of your friends outside when the time comes, but the baggage car is going to be our first stop."

Chapter 2

Before she and Ki left the coach with the robber, Jessie turned to reassure the passengers.

"Just stay in your seats," she cautioned them. "Don't worry if you hear some shooting." Then, more for the benefit of their prisoner than the passengers, she added, "We're trying to capture these robbers alive, but if they decide not to give up, and start shooting, I'll have to shoot back."

Then, seeing Ki waiting at the front vestibule door, she prodded the outlaw with the revolver muzzle, and they followed Ki out of the coach.

Before opening the door into the baggage car, Ki turned and said to their prisoner, "Don't try to warn your friend in there. Jessie meant what she just said. And since you're the first one who'll be going into the baggage car, you'll more than likely take the first bullet."

"You won't have to worry about me," the outlaw answered meekly. "I'd a sight rather be alive and in jail than in a coffin under six feet of dirt."

"Go ahead, then," Jessie told the man, prodding him in the back with the muzzle of her revolver. "Open the door."

Every move showing his reluctance, the bandit moved forward when Ki stepped aside. He moved the door into the baggage car, and over his shoulder Ki saw the robber in the car. The man was kneeling beside the big iron-bound express box, trying to pry its lid open with a short piece of strap-iron.

When he heard the click of the doorknob the man at the strongbox looked around. His move galvanized Ki into action. Pushing aside the robber in front of him, who still stood with his hand on the doorknob, Ki dived toward the opposite end of the baggage car. Turning in midair, he landed on his feet and whirled in an *obi-geri* attack, one foot extended as he twirled on the other foot to sweep the kneeling bandit to the floor with a sweeping *ashigatana* kick.

As he toppled, the outlaw tried to draw his hip-holstered revolver, but Ki had only begun his attack. He dived for the sprawled-out bandit, who by now had wrestled his pistol from its holster, and sent the weapon flying from the man's hand with a sweeping *oi-tsuki* punch. Ki's momentum carried him forward, and he reached the outlaw in a split second. The man was still trying to get to his feet, and Ki added a *chudan* punch to his initial attack. The heel of his palm, almost as hard as a chunk of iron, swept up in a blow that landed on the man's chin and knocked the scrabbling bandit backward. Landing limply on the floor, he lay sprawled out, unconscious.

Meanwhile, Jessie was dealing with the other outlaw. He'd tried to take advantage of the distraction created by Ki's attack on the man at the strongbox by turning quickly,

14

his hand outstretched, reaching for the revolver Jessie held. Although she was not as adept as Ki in the martial arts of the Orient, he'd taught Jessie enough of the basics to give her an edge, which she used to counter the outlaw's clumsy effort.

Swinging the revolver out of his reach, Jessie carried the weapon's arc into a semicircular sweep downward that enabled her to evade his clumsy lunge. As she brought up the revolver at the end of its compact arc, she angled it to strike the outlaw's jaw. When the weapon's backstrap landed on his chin the man's teeth cracked and he sagged to the floor, as unconscious as his companion.

"That takes care of the bandits on the train," Jessie said. Her voice was as casual as though she was making a remark about having taken a pleasant stroll across the prairie. "But we still have the three outside to think about."

"We'll be able to deal with them one at a time," Ki told her. "When the ones we've put out of commission don't show up, the leader's going to send his extra man in here to see what's happening to delay them."

"Then all we have to do—" Jessie began, but broke off when a sudden rattling, banging noise broke out from somewhere in the coach.

It took them only a few seconds to locate the source of the noise; both Jessie and Ki had been too busy putting the outlaws out of action to take even the most cursory look at the coach's interior. Now, a quick scanning glance disclosed the wooden locker or compartment that had been built into one corner of the coach. It extended from floor to ceiling, and its door was closed by a simple hasp, with an unlocked padlock securing it.

Ki reached the compartment in two quick steps and lifted the padlock from the eye of the hasp. The door swung open, and a man wearing the standard coat and pants of blue serge that trainmen favored stepped out into the car. His head was bare, his sparse brown hair tousled, and a red weal ran from his brow-line to one eye. Shaking his head groggily, the man stared for a moment at Jessie and Ki, then at the sprawled forms of the two unconscious outlaws. Then he nodded and looked again at Jessie and Ki.

"You're in the rear coach," he said. "Ticketed to the Circle Star whistlestop."

"That's right," Jessie agreed. "I'm Jessica Starbuck, and this is Ki, who—" She paused for a moment, trying to explain Ki's status to the railroader, and settled for saying, "—who works at the Circle Star."

"Looks like you did a pretty good job putting the robbers down," the trainman said. "They didn't give me much of a chance to do anything. Those two on the floor came busting through the door just as soon as the drag slowed down. One of them jumped me before I knew what was happening, and the other one whacked me a good one on the head. At first I didn't know what was going on when I woke up there in the tool locker, but it didn't take me long to figure it out. Then I heard a ruckus and then you two started talking. Thanks for getting me outta trouble."

"We're not out of trouble yet," Jessie told him. "There are three more of the gang outside. Ki and I were just starting to plan a way to capture them without giving them a chance to do any more shooting when you started knocking."

"We don't have much time," Ki put in quickly. "If one or both of these men don't show up outside in a very few minutes, the others will be coming aboard the train to find out what's gone wrong."

"There's two new Winchesters over there in the tool locker," the brakeman said. "I couldn't manage to get at

16

them because with me inside it was too crowded."

"I suppose you can handle a rifle?" Jessie asked.

"Sure can. Grew up with one on the farm where I was born," the railroader answered. "You sound like you've got some idea about what we'd best do."

Jessie nodded. "I have. But we'd better tie up these two men we've captured and gag them so they can't warn the other outlaws. I hope there's some rope in that place where you were locked up."

"There is," the brakie replied. "And some wipe-rags, too; they'll do to make gags out of. I'll get them and the rope, and I guess I'd better fetch those rifles at the same time."

"Yes, we may need them before this is over," Jessie agreed as the railroader started for the locker. Then she turned to Ki and went on, "You remember what this outlaw over here said about the two men at the locomotive, Ki. We don't have much time to spare, because one of them is going to be coming on the train pretty soon to find out what's happened to the ones we've captured."

"I've been thinking the same thing," Ki replied. "But we've got two choices, Jessie. We can—" He broke off as the brakeman returned. He carried a bundle of rags and a coil of rope in one hand, and was struggling to keep the two rifles from sliding out from under his other arm. Ki said quickly, "Here, let me help. You tie one of them; I'll tie up the other."

"And while you're doing that, I'll check these rifles," Jessie volunteered.

As they began working, Ki went on, "I can't see that we have a great deal of choice if we want to capture all three of those outlaws who're still outside. We'll just have to wait here until one of them comes aboard the train. When we've put him out of action, we can deal with the other

17

two. Since they're on opposite sides of the train, we ought to be able to take them one at a time."

"That's about how it looks to me," Jessie agreed. "If we can move fast enough and take them by surprise, one at a time, it'll save a lot of gunplay."

Before Ki could reply, the knob of the door at the front end of the coach rattled. He leaped to his feet and started for the door, but it opened while he was still eight or ten feet away from it. A swarthy man, roughly dressed, came through the door and took a step into the coach before he saw his two unconscious companions stretched out on the floor. Jessie was still knotting the rope that held one of the outlaws, and the brakeman was busy completing the lashings that secured the other.

"What in hell's name—" the newcomer began, his hand dropping to his holstered revolver as he took in the unexpected scene that met his eyes.

Jessie had holstered her Colt. She reached for the rifle that lay on the floor by her feet, but while she was still bringing it to her shoulder Ki had begun his own attack. Propelled by his muscular legs, he'd launched himself into a long leap toward the door at the first clicking of the knob.

Before the surprised outlaw could bring up his pistol, Ki's leap had carried him close enough to the newcomer for him to lash out with a *yokotobi-geri* kick that knocked the pistol from the newcomer's hand before he could level it.

As the weapon clattered to the floor, Ki's other foot was cutting through the air in a second kick. His sandal-clad heel smashed into the outlaw's chin with a solid *thwack*. The man staggered backward, his head striking the door-frame with enough force to stun him. It was child's play for Ki to finish the job. He landed solidly on his feet beside the half-conscious outlaw and thrust his arm forward in an

18

oi-tsuki punch that finished what the outlaw's collision with the doorframe had begun.

As his smash into the doorframe sent the breath from his lungs in a declining sigh, the bandit slid down the wall beside the door, his revolver dropping from his hand as he sagged to the floor. Ki kicked the newcomer's pistol to one side and dragged him to where Jessie and the brakeman were finishing their job of tying the other two outlaws.

"I think he'll stay unconscious long enough for you to tie him up, too," Ki told Jessie. "And now we've only got two more of the gang to take care of."

"We'll have to move fast," Jessie said, looping the rope around the unconscious outlaw's wrists, then yanking it down to lash his ankles together. "I'd say the best way to get them at about the same time is for you to jump the leader from the top of the locomotive cab while I go down to the other end of the train and cover the second lookout."

"They won't be looking for us overhead," Ki said, nodding. "Let's get busy before these others come to and start yelling."

"I'll stay here and keep 'em quiet," the brakeman volunteered. "From what I've seen, you two have worked together before on jobs like this one. I'd just be in your way."

"Try to keep these prisoners quiet, if you can," Jessie told the railroader over her shoulder as she started toward the door to join Ki. "With any luck, we'll be able to put the other two out of action before they come to, especially if they're not spooked by hearing any noise from inside the train here."

When Jessie joined Ki between the baggage car and tender, he'd already started up the coal-car's back ladder. Jessie wasted no time in mounting the ladder on the end of the baggage car. She was careful not to climb too high, but bent forward and wormed her way up the last two rungs as she straightened out along the catwalk that ran down the middle of the car's rounded top. Then she began inching toward the back.

Below, she could see the creased crown of the lookout's tall Stetson moving as he sat his horse beside the tracks, looking first in one direction and then the other as he scanned the side of the motionless train. Glancing toward the locomotive, she also saw Ki. He was moving in the same fashion that she was, lying flat on the arch of the locomotive cab and propelling himself with his knees and elbows.

Before she turned her eyes away, Ki looked over his shoulder toward her. He held up his hand, his fingers outspread, closed the hand into a fist then opened it again. It was a signal he and Jessie always used when they needed to keep silent. She nodded and began inching closer to the rider on the grade below, knowing that Ki intended to launch his attack against the outlaw leader in ten seconds, counting mentally to be sure that she would begin her attack on the lookout at the same time.

Eight of Jessie's ten seconds had passed by the time she reached a position a few feet away from the spot where the outlaw lookout had posted himself. She glanced back once, and saw Ki crouched on all fours, ready to leap. Her mind ticked off the two remaining seconds, and then she turned away from Ki, intent now only on her own part of the job at hand.

Leaping to her feet she took quick aim, gambling that the sights of the Winchester were accurate. Then she triggered off a slug that went through the peak of the long vertical Texas crease that pulled the Stetson's high crown to a point six or eight inches above its wearer's skull. The hat flew off as the rifle bullet drove through the thick, tough felt.

Instinctively, the outlaw whose head the Stetson had adorned raised his hand toward his half-bald skull, but a second before his hand reached his hairline his delayed reaction sent his eyes upward, where he saw Jessie standing on the top of the coach, levering a fresh round into the Winchester's magazine. Jessie swung the muzzle until she had the outlaw's eyes in her sights.

"Just freeze your right hand where it is," she said. "And leave your left hand on your reins. I wouldn't have any regrets at all if I had to pull this trigger."

Jessie's calm tone and her hard voice carried an authority that got home to the startled bandit at once. He held both hands carefully motionless while he gazed at her, his jaw dropping incredulously. Before he could recover from his surprise and begin asking questions, Ki's shout broke the silence that had followed the shot and Jessie's command.

"I've got the boss outlaw," he called. "And I'd guess your man's either dead or has his hands up. Suppose you bring him around the front of the train, and we'll figure out what to do with the bunch of them."

"My man's still alive, and I don't want to shoot him unless he plays the fool," Jessie shouted in reply. "You'd better send one of the men from the engine to lead him around the engine on his horse. I can keep my rifle on him while he's moving."

Within a few moments an overall-clad man dropped off the engine and walked along beside the baggage car until he could reach the reins of the subdued bandit. He looked up at Jessie, who was still standing motionless on top of the baggage-car, covering the outlaw with the rifle.

"Just keep this fellow in your sights, lady, while I lead

21

his horse around to where that Chinaman's got his boss," the railroad man said. "It won't take us long to figure out a way to keep 'em safe."

"You're in charge of the train," Jessie told him. "Ki and I will do whatever you think best."

"Well, these cussed outlaws killed the conductor, so that puts the engineer in charge," the man said as he took the reins of the outlaw's mount and started leading it toward the engine. "It looks like we'll have to back up to Uvalde. We'll lose a lot of time, but that's the closest place where we can turn 'em over to the law."

"That's what you should do, then," Jessie replied. "We'll be glad to go along and help, even if it means losing a day."

"I'm certainly glad to see that little depot," Jessie told Ki, nodding toward the little depot and the corrals beyond it, when the train began slowing to the accompaniment of a few creaks from the swaying coaches and occasional squeal of brake-shoes. At last, with a final hiss of steam from the engine's cylinders, it came to a full stop in front of the little station that marked the Circle Star whistlestop.

It was mid-morning of the day following the thwarted holdup, and they'd had a busy fourteen hours. In Uvalde, Jessie and Ki had answered questions and signed sworn affidavits for the county sheriff as well as for a handful of I&GN detectives and officials who'd been sent on a special train from San Antonio when word of the attempted robbery had been wired on the railroad telegraph to the main office.

Daylight had been creeping up the eastern sky when the train had resumed its interrupted progress, and after their sleepless night, both Jessie and Ki had slept during most of the remainder of their journey home. Now, Jessie looked through the coach window at the corral that stood a short distance from the depot.

"Seeing Sun over there makes me feel better," she went on. "It'll be a real pleasure to get back in the saddle again."

"It'll be more of a pleasure to get back to the Circle Star, where it's reasonably quiet," Ki told her. "Luckily, we don't have to worry about starting to gather the market herd for at least another couple of months."

"Yes, I'll enjoy some quiet days, too," Jessie agreed. "For a few minutes yesterday I got the feeling that we were back battling the cartel again."

She and Ki had stood up while they talked. They'd started moving down the aisle toward the coach door, but their progress was slowed by having to pause at almost every seat to acknowledge the greetings and words of thanks from the passengers who'd been aboard during the aborted holdup. At last they'd reached the door and stepped off to the station platform.

Jessie had eyes only for the corral, where Ki's pony and Sun were waiting. Alerted to her presence by that inexplicable sixth sense so many domestic animals have, the sense that binds them to a much-loved master or mistress, Sun had started prancing almost before the train came to a full stop. Now, when he saw Jessie, the big palomino neighed and reared up on his hind legs. His forefeet began flailing the air and his snorts were louder than they'd been before, when he'd only sensed that Jessie was close by.

"I'll leave you to pick up the mail and take care of the luggage, Ki," she said. "All that I need to take to the ranch is my small dressing-case. We'll leave the big suitcases for one of the hands to pick up later in the buckboard. Right now, I'm going over to the corral and see Sun."

Ki disappeared into the vest-pocket–sized depot. Jessie ran down the platform's steps and hurried to the corral. Sun had stopped neighing now, and had moved to the side of the enclosure from which Jessie was approaching. The sunlight glowed in the golden strands of his flowing mane, and he began pawing the ground with one front hoof, nickering eagerly. Jessie stopped at the corral fence and patted the big stallion's outthrust muzzle.

"You've been lonesome, haven't you, Sun?" Jessie asked softly as she ran her hand up the short fuzzy hair of his muzzle. "We'll have a good run or two on the way back to the Circle Star, and an even better one tomorrow. I need to shake the city-smell out of my lungs just as badly as you need the exercise."

★

Chapter 3

Sun had grown calmer during the few minutes that passed while Jessie walked from the station to the corral, and the big stallion relaxed into his normal behavior after he'd felt the touch of Jessie's hand. He was standing quietly when Ki came up, carrying a mail-pouch in one hand and Jessie's dressing-case in the other.

"It'll only take me a minute to saddle Sun and my own pony, and we'll be heading for home," he told Jessie. "Oh, yes—the station agent said there's a telegram and a special delivery letter too, in the mailbag. You might want to look at them while I'm getting the horses saddled."

Ki handed Jessie the mail-pouch, then ducked through the bars of the pole-fence that formed the corral. Jessie opened the flap of the pouch. It was packed with letters, but most of them were the routine reports of the managers responsible for the day-to-day operations of the many Starbuck enterprises that Jessie had inherited from her father.

She skimmed quickly through the envelopes, which bore the imprints of banks and brokerage houses in several cities, of mines and lumbering and shipping firms, of railroads and lawyers and men prominent in Washington as well as several statehouses.

At last she found the mail to which Ki had referred, a small yellow envelope which contained the telegram and the large square envelope of expensive vellum stationery that bore the special delivery stamp. She opened the telegram first, and as she read the single line on the flimsy yellow paper a puzzled frown formed on her face.

"Mother and I will arrive on Tuesday," the message read. Jessie's frown grew even more perplexed when she looked at the totally unfamiliar name, "Steven Chalmers," with which the message was signed. Still holding the cryptic telegram, Jessie turned the big envelope in her hands to inspect its back flap. Her frown vanished almost completely, leaving only a puzzled crease in her brow as she read the return address engraved on the flap: "Lucinda Barrows Chalmers, The Elms, Holyoke, Mass."

This was a name that stirred old memories in Jessie's mind, but it also presented its own puzzle. Hurriedly, she ripped the flap open and took out the double-folded page of expensive stationery. The letter was written in exquisite Spencerian script, and a smile grew on Jessie's face as she scanned the flowing lines:

My dear Jessica,

Although for several years we have both been remiss in our correspondence, I am sure that at least one of the several invitations you extended to me during your days at Miss Booth's Academy must still remain in effect. Now that I am widowed and my responsibilities have diminished to the administration

26

of my late husband's estate, I am at last free to accept your kind invitation to visit you on your ranch.

I will be accompanied by my stepson, Steven, who like me has never had an opportunity to explore the western attractions of our native land. We will set out from Boston within the week, and I will notify you of the date of our arrival by telegraph.

If for any reason you would view our visit as incommodious, you have only to write or telegraph and we will make other arrangements. I am looking forward to seeing you. With all best wishes and looking forward to a pleasant reunion, most sincerely,

Lucinda Barrows Chalmers.

Jessie was re-reading the letter for a second time, connecting it at last with the puzzling telegram, when Ki led Sun and his own pony up to the fence. He looked at Jessie with a small frown and asked, "Was there bad news in the telegram or in that special delivery letter?"

Shaking her head, Jessie said, "No. Not bad news, but a bit of a surprise. This is Saturday, isn't it, Ki?"

"Yes, of course. Why?"

"Things have been happening so fast that I seem to have lost track of the days," Jessie told him with a mock-serious grin. She looked at the postmark on the letter and the date on the telegram and frowned thoughtfully before going on, "This letter is from Miss Barrows, Ki. You might not remember her, but she was my favorite teacher at Miss Booth's Academy."

"I remember her quite well, even though I only saw her two or three times when I went with Alex to visit you there."

"She's coming to the Circle Star for a visit, Ki. Goodness knows, I invited her several times when I was still in school, before—" Jessie paused. Her face clouded briefly, but then she went on. "—before Alex was murdered. Of course you know the rest of it; how I had to leave Miss Booth's and try to pick up all the threads left after Alex was killed. I've thought about Miss Barrows now and then when business took us East, but there was never enough time to stop for a visit."

"When do you expect her?" Ki asked.

"On Tuesday, I suppose," Jessie replied. "She wrote that she'd send me a telegram giving the exact date when she'd get here, and there was a telegram from—" She frowned and went on thoughtfully, "I suppose her stepson sent it."

"Where was the telegram sent from?" Ki went on.

"New Orleans. And it was dated last Thursday, so that'd mean they'll be here in just three more days."

"They?" Ki frowned.

"In her letter Miss Barrows said that her stepson would be with her, and the signature on the telegram was Steven Chalmers's. Miss Barrows's notepaper gives her name as Chalmers, so I'd imagine that she must've married a man named Chalmers who already had a son, and she's adopted the son, or whatever people do in such cases."

"I wouldn't know that myself, but it makes sense." Ki nodded. "It needn't bother you, though, Jessie. We've entertained guests at the Circle Star often enough."

"Oh, it doesn't really bother me," Jessie replied. "I'm just still surprised at having gotten a letter from Miss Barrows, or Mrs. Chalmers, as she is now."

"We'll have plenty of time to get things ready," Ki assured her. "Now, suppose we start for home. We can figure out all the details later."

"I certainly hope nothing's happened to change their plans," Jessie said as the westbound train came into sight around the curve.

She and Ki were standing beside the carriage Jessie had selected to use when meeting their visitors. It was one which Alex had designed to accommodate visitors to the Circle Star, a six-seat vehicle modeled after the English "carryall," but light enough to be drawn by a single horse. Though Jessie seldom used the wagon, she'd had two of the Circle Star's horse wranglers drag it out of the big barn where it had been gathering dust and give it a thorough cleaning. Its brass fittings, long, black, highly-varnished bed and high, red-painted wheels, and its opulent leather upholstered seats, shone in the bright sunlight of the cloudless morning.

"Don't worry," Ki assured her. "If they'd missed making connections or been delayed, they'd have sent you a telegram."

"Of course they would," Jessie agreed. "And I don't know why the idea of seeing Miss Barrows again keeps bothering me. I guess it's because she seemed so impressively dignified all the time when I was in school."

"You'll be meeting under different circumstances now," Ki told her. "And I'm sure you'll enjoy seeing her again. I remember how you used to sing her praises when you'd come home to the ranch for your summer vacations."

"Maybe it's because I'm not a schoolgirl any more," Jessie suggested. "But at least we'll be meeting on my home grounds now instead of the Academy, where that formal New England atmosphere tended to impress me so much."

By now the train was braking to a stop in front of the

little depot. The baggage-car door slid open and the baggage-master began carrying suitcases from the car to pile on the depot platform. Jessie paid little attention to the luggage. Her eyes were fixed on the conductor, who was standing at the door of the passenger coach. He extended a hand to the young man who came out, but the passenger waved the offered arm aside and turned to stand beside the door across from the conductor.

"That looks like one of your guests," Ki said. "I'll wait here while you go meet them."

Jessie started for the door of the railroad coach. Her eyebrows lifted when she recognized the woman who appeared next in the coach door. She was an impressive figure, tall and stately, with an oval face distinguished by a slightly-too-small aquiline nose, full lips, high cheekbones, deep violet-blue eyes, and a firm jawline. She wore a dark brown serge traveling suit that glistened with newness, and a silk turban-style hat adorned with a single tan-colored feather plume that was secured to the hat with an elaborate pin sparkling with a half-dozen good-sized diamonds.

For a moment Jessie stared, speechless, trying to reconcile the woman as the Miss Barrows she remembered from her days at the Academy. That Miss Barrows had seemed much thinner and much older, and Jessie had never seen her wear anything except the simple full-cut dress of dark gray serge and a white high-necked blouse unadorned by any jewelry—the costume which was so commonplace as to be almost a uniform for the school's teachers.

Then the alighting passenger saw Jessie and smiled, and now Jessie felt at home in her presence, for the smile brought back the sympathetic teacher who'd been the favorite among all of her instructors at Miss Booth's Academy. She ran forward, her arms open, and Miss Barrows met her with her own outstretched arms.

"Jessica!" she exclaimed. "Jessica Starbuck! You've turned into a woman instead of the schoolgirl I used to teach, but I'd have known you anywhere!"

"And I'd have known you, too, Miss Barrows," Jessie replied. Then, catching her tongue-slip, she quickly corrected it. "Mrs. Chalmers, I should've said, but it may take me a little while to get used to your married name. Anyhow, you know that whatever name I might call you by, you're certainly welcome to Texas and to the Circle Star!"

"I hope there's not as much to the Circle Star as there is to Texas," Mrs. Chalmers said, and smiled. "I thought we were never going to get here! And so did Steven—" She paused, her mouth still open, then went on quickly, "And I'm doing exactly what I tried to teach you not to do in welcoming guests." Turning to the young man who'd been standing beside the car door watching them, she went on, "Jessica, allow me to present my adopted son, Steven Chalmers. Steven, Miss Jessica Starbuck, whom I've mentioned to you so many times."

"I'm honored, Miss Starbuck," the young man said, taking Jessie's extended hand and bowing over it. "I've heard so much about you from mother since we started planning this trip that I feel I already know you."

"Mr. Chalmers." Jessie nodded. "I'm glad to have both you and your mother as my guests on the Circle Star. But we'd better put off any more conversation until later, because the train's going to be moving soon, and it might be a good idea to see that none of your luggage has been left in the baggage car."

"Oh, I took care of that earlier," young Chalmers said. "Long before the conductor called our stop, I went into the baggage car and made sure that all of our suitcases were placed in front of the door for unloading."

"Then I'll get Ki to bring up the wagon and we'll load

31

them and start for the ranch," Jessie replied. She waved to Ki and gestured toward the pile of suitcases on the platform. He nodded, took the wagon-horse's bridle and began leading it toward the depot just as the locomotive's whistle sounded and the train rolled away.

"Exactly where is your ranch?" Miss Barrows asked as Jessie turned to her again. "I don't see a single house—just this little dinky depot, and the same barren country that we've been watching since we left the last town."

"Texas distances take a bit of getting used to," Jessie said. "The ranch begins at that fence just beyond the depot, but we'll be riding almost four hours before we can see the Circle Star headquarters buildings."

"Four hours!" Steven exclaimed. "It would seem to me that you'd want your ranch buildings closer to the railroad."

"My father chose the site for our home place," Jessie explained. "He had his own reasons for not wanting to be too near the railroad line. Besides, it's much more convenient to have the ranch headquarters near the center of our range."

"Are you saying that you own the land for another four hours' ride beyond your home and your ranch headquarters?" he asked, belatedly aware that he'd been staring at Jessie with his jaws agape.

"It'd be more like six hours," Jessie answered. "And a bit more than twice that far to the side boundaries on the east and west."

Steven frowned thoughtfully for a moment, then said, "But that's as far as it is from Holyoke to Boston, Miss Starbuck! Your ranch must be almost as big as Massachussetts!"

"Yes, it is." Jessie nodded. "Not quite as big, but it doesn't lack much. And we won't get to the main house until time for a late supper, but I've brought along a picnic basket, so we won't be hungry."

"I'm having trouble visualizing your ranch, Jessie," Mrs. Chalmers put in. "I had no idea it was so terribly large."

"There are some others in Texas that are even larger," Jessie told her. "Land's not at the premium here that it is in the East." She saw that Ki had begun to load the suitcases onto the wagon and went on, "Suppose we give Ki a hand in getting your bags loaded."

"Ki?" Steven frowned. "That sounds like an Oriental name."

"It is," Jessie said as she turned and started toward the wagon. "My father and Ki were together for a number of years, even before I was born. I'm very lucky that he's stayed with me since Alex's death."

"I gather that his status is something more than a servant, then?" Mrs. Chalmers asked.

"Very much more," Jessie nodded. "Don't you remember that when Alex visited me at the academy Ki was always with him?"

"Yes, but I just assumed that he was your father's manservant. I didn't realize that they were—well, I suppose friends is the word I'm looking for."

"Ki's my friend, of course, just as he was Alex's, and he's also invaluable in helping me to take care of the businesses that Alex left me."

They reached the wagon just as Ki dropped to the ground to lift the last suitcase into the wagon. Jessie understood at once why he'd chosen to hurry the loading and leave the platform; Ki wished to be out of handshaking distance when introduced to Steven Chalmers to avoid any possibility of a mutually embarrassing moment when introduced. She made a mental note to begin as quickly as possible to cure any diffidence on Ki's part and to acquaint Steven with their relationship.

She went on. "Ki, I'm sure you'll remember Mrs. Chalmers from your visits to the academy with Alex. And this is her son, Steven."

Ki's bow saluted both the new arrivals, and as he straightened up he said, "Of course I remember. I am honored to be able to greet you again, Mrs. Chalmers." He nodded to Steven and added, "And to meet you, Mr. Chalmers." With a gesture that took in both the wagon and the station platform, he went on, "I'll pull up a few feet to get closer, then you can step into the wagon without having to descend to the ground."

Jessie saw at once that there'd be no better time to bring Ki and young Chalmers into close contact. She said, "Steven, suppose you ride with Ki in the front seat. Perhaps you might even like to take the reins for a while." Turning to Mrs. Chalmers, she went on, "There's not a great deal of scenery to look at on the way, so you and I will be able to talk about the days at the Academy and catch up on everything that's happened since then."

"You've probably been wondering about the most important thing that's happened to me," Mrs. Chalmers began as Ki slapped the reins over the horse's back and the wagon began moving away from the station. "That would be my marriage, of course." She stopped short and looked at Jessie with the ghost of an almost-formed frown, then asked, "I've often wondered if you ever got married, Jessica."

"For one thing, I've been too busy," Jessie said lightly. "And for another, I haven't found a man yet whom I'd want to live with the rest of my life. But *you* married late, if you'll excuse me for mentioning it."

"Yes." Mrs. Chalmers nodded. "And I'm very glad I did, even if I had only a few years with my late husband.

But before I tell you about myself, Jessica, let me remind you that you're not a schoolgirl now, and I'm not your teacher. I hope I'm your friend, so please don't follow the rule I taught you at the Academy. I intend to keep calling you Jessica, and I'll be greatly obliged if you'll call me Lucy, which I much prefer to Lucinda."

"I'll make a bargain with you," Jessie proposed. "I won't call you either Mrs. Chalmers or Lucinda if you'll call me Jessie instead of Jessica."

"Agreed. Now, shall I tell you my story first, or shall I listen to yours?"

"I think you know my story better than I do yours," Jessie replied. "And of course I want to know all about what you've been doing during the years since we last saw one another. But let's wait to have a long talk until we get you and Steven settled in and we can spend all the time we need without being interrupted."

While Jessie talked, Lucinda Chalmers had been eyeing the expanse of prairie that surrounded them. Wherever she looked, the horizon seemed to be infinitely distant, the waving grama grass broken only by an occasional isolated clump of mesquite at a waterhole. The trail along which the wagon rolled was the only sign visible on the landscape that at some time people passed this way.

"I certainly don't see anything out here that would be likely to interrupt us," she told Jessie. "Why, except for those little patches of brush there's not a single thing in sight anywhere. I know you must have a house some-where, and I guess this ranch or farm or whatever you call it must grow something, but I don't see any crops coming up, or any way that you'd get the water to grow them."

"Our crop's cattle," Jessie replied. "We'll probably catch sight of one of the herds before we get to the main house. But you're right, there aren't any streams. We have waterholes, of course, but they're hard to see until you get within a few feet of them. They're not terribly big, and only a few of them are fed by springs. But even if the land looks dried-out, we do get enough rain to keep most of them filled."

Steven and Ki had exchanged only a few offhand remarks since they'd started. Now, Steven turned to Jessie and asked, "What about the Indians? Do they give you much trouble?"

"Why, there aren't any Indians within a hundred miles of here!" Jessie exclaimed. "The nearest ones you'll find are more than two hundred miles away, and they're peaceful Pueblo tribes who have a settlement north of El Paso, in New Mexico."

"Well, I'm glad to hear that!" Mrs. Chalmers exclaimed. "I'll confess that I don't know much about this part of the country, Jessie. And I'm not sure I'd like it, being so far away from everything."

"That's one of the reasons Alex chose this spot," Jessie said. "He was involved in so many businesses that he needed to be isolated from everywhere now and then."

"And you really do like it, too?" Steven asked.

"Very much indeed," Jessie replied. "When I have to make a business trip, I'm always glad to get back. But you'll see when we get to the main house that even if we're isolated here, we do manage to enjoy a fairly civilized existence."

Chapter 4

Against the darkening blue of the cloudless after-sunset sky, the buildings that formed the Circle Star's headquarters stood out in bold relief as the carryall reached the top of the low rise and the wagon's occupants got their first look at them.

At one side of the built-up area, the high, blocky walls of the two-story main house, spaced a little apart from the other buildings, towered like a modestly-sized castle above the cluster of smaller wooden structures. These included the bunkhouse, the cookshack and dining-room, the black-smith's shop, and the barns. The pole fences that enclosed the horse corrals and the walkways between them gave the impression that the entire cluster formed a small village.

At this late hour, with darkness only a half-hour or so away, most of the ranch hands were already in the bunk-house. Lamplight glowed from its windows, and in the windows of the long, narrow building that housed the dining-room and kitchen. Two or three of the hands were visible in the walkways between the corrals, and a few more lounged in front of the yawning double doors of the main barn. But the big main house was dark.

When they got their first glimpse of the ranch buildings, both Lucy Chalmers and Steven gasped in surprise, and when Lucy had recovered from the first shock of what she was looking at, she said, "Why, Jessie, I knew your ranch must be nice, but I certainly didn't look for it to be anything as elaborate as this!"

"I didn't either," Steven volunteered. "It's so big! It's almost as big as some of the little old villages we still have in the New England states."

"Well, the Circle Star's a long way from being the biggest ranch in Texas," Jessie told them. "And even the biggest Texas ranches don't cover as much ground as some of the old Spanish grants in New Mexico and California. Of course, this isn't all of it. We've got a dozen line shacks scattered around, and if you'd add them to what we have here at the main house, then it really might look like a little town."

"What's a line shack?" Steven asked.

Ki answered before Jessie could speak. "Just a little shanty big enough for a couple of bunks and a monkey stove. When the men are out tallying or gathering strays on the range farthest from the bunkhouse here, they'll stay overnight in them to save having to pick their way home in the dark."

"Why do you call them line shacks, then?" Steven frowned.

"Because they're usually on the edge of the spread, close to the Circle Star property line," Ki explained.

"Now tell me what a monkey stove is," young Chalmers said.

"That's what the hands call a little upright stove, not much bigger around than the stovepipe," Ki replied.

"Why are they called monkey stoves?" Steven persisted.

Ki shrugged. "No one seems to know. I don't know anybody who could answer that question for you."

While they talked, the carryall had covered the short distance to the main house. Ki reined in. Ed Wright, the Circle Star foreman, was already walking across the narrow stretch of beaten earth between the main house and the cookshack. He lifted his forefinger to the wide brim of his tall-crowned, tan Stetson as he stopped and faced Jessie.

"Is there anything me or the fellows can do, Miss Jessie?" he asked.

"Nothing except putting the carryall in the barn, Ed," Jessie replied. "There's no hurry. Ki will unload their luggage first." Turning to her guests, she went on. "This is Ed Wright, our foreman. Ed, these are the guests we've been looking for, Mrs. Chalmers and her son, Steven." As Wright doffed his hat and bowed in the general direction of the newcomers, Jessie added, "If you ever need anything when Ki or I aren't around, Ed's the man to see."

Nodding as he spoke, Wright seconded Jessie's remark. "Any way I can help you folks, just let me know. Now, I'd better go get one of the boys to move this rig and unhitch the horse after you finish unloading."

After Wright had moved out of earshot, Lucy Chalmers said to Jessie, "You know, Jessie, I'm not sure that I approve of the familiarity you allow your servants. Have you forgotten all the social graces that you learned at the Academy?"

"Out here, ranch hands aren't servants, Lucy," Jessie replied. "They're skilled workmen who very often risk getting hurt or even killed when they're doing their jobs. When Ki and I are away, Ed Wright's in full charge of the

Circle Star, and even when we're here I seldom give him any orders. He and I both know that we'll have to start the tally tomorrow, but I haven't told him to, because I know he'll just go ahead and do it."

"If 'tally' means out here what it does in the East, that must be when you're counting your cows," Steven put in.

"Not cows, Steven," Jessie told him. "Steers."

"If they're steers, why aren't your workmen called steerboys instead of cowboys?" Steven frowned.

"Now, that's a question I don't think anybody can answer, Steve," Jessie replied. "It's like asking you or anyone else from New England why lobstermen aren't called lobster fishers."

"I see your point." Steven nodded. "And I'll try not to ask any more foolish questions, Jessie." He turned to Ki and went on, "Here. Let me give you a hand with our luggage. I'm beginning to get the idea that here in the West drones don't belong in the beehives."

"You're sure that you're not too tired after your trip to stay up and talk?" Jessie asked Lucy Chalmers.

"Of course I'm a bit tired, but sitting here isn't going to tire me any more," Lucy answered. She looked around the room that had been Alex's study and was Jessie's favorite among all the rooms in the Circle Star's sprawling main house. "This is a very restful room, Jessie. I can understand why you like it as much as you told me you do."

Jessie contented herself with a nod in response to Lucy's remark. She saw that her guest was examining their surroundings more closely, and realizing that the examination was her way of gaining time before revealing whatever was on her mind. Jessie herself was relaxed as always in her favorite room.

After their late supper, Ki and Steven had chosen to

remain in the big high-ceilinged livingroom and chat in front of the huge slate-gray stone fireplace which held the almost life-sized oil portrait of the mother Jessie had never seen. On its floor of polished oaken boards stood heavy furniture that was scaled to match the room's dimensions. Tables held kerosene lamps that cast their glow over a pair of massive leather-upholstered divans and wide matching armchairs.

In contrast to the cavernous and more formal living room it was small in size, and had been planned by Alex for his study. The study was a contrast to the living-room. It was furnished a bit more simply, with a sofa and two chairs of matching leather upholstery, but its most attention-getting piece of furniture was the old, scarred rolltop desk that had been Alex's first purchase when he opened the little Oriental curio shop in San Francisco—his first business venture. One wall of the study was lined with crowded bookshelves, and in addition to the rarely-used fireplace there was a small baseburner with isinglass set into its pierced door.

"Yes," Lucy went on, "this is a room where we can talk."

"I've always found it to be," Jessie said. "I've spent a great deal of my time in here, trying to think of all the things I had to do in settling the business affairs that Alex had been working on before he was murdered. You remember how upset I was, Lucy, when I got Ki's telegram telling me that my father had been murdered and that I must hurry back here."

Jessie had already resolved to say nothing to her guests about the long series of battles she and Ki had fought before they had broken the power of the criminal European cartel that had been her father's enemy, and which had brought about his untimely death. She went on. "After I

41

finally learned enough to supervise Alex's estate, we settled in here at the ranch."

"And from what you've said, your ranch must require a great deal of attention," Mrs. Chalmers said.

Jessie nodded. "I keep busy. But it's a slack time now on the Circle Star. You couldn't have timed your visit better."

"That does relieve my mind, Jessie. Because in addition to being anxious to see you again—I never did tell you while you were a student that you were my favorite, because becoming too friendly with the girls was against the Academy rules."

"Now, that's one of the nicest things I've heard." Jessie smiled. "And I never did make any secret about you being my very favorite teacher."

"No, you didn't, though I sensed it and was quite flattered. But to get back to my story, I want to tell you something at once, something about which I'm a bit ashamed."

"I can't imagine you doing anything that would embarrass you or anyone else!"

Her voice very sober now, Lucy Chalmers went on. "Jessie, in addition to wanting to see you again, I have a problem that I'd like to talk with you about. But the details can wait—they *must* wait—until I've told you other things that contribute to my problem."

"Suppose you just start at the beginning, then," Jessie suggested.

Mrs. Chalmers nodded. "Yes, that's what I need to do." She sat silently for a moment, then continued. "I couldn't go into a lot of detail in my letter to you, Jessie. I met my late husband through mutual friends. Luckily, Arthur was as attracted to me as I was to him. He was a widower, and Steven was old enough to accept the idea of a stepmother, so Arthur and I had no problems after we were married. I left the Academy at once, of course, and we had some very happy years. I won't dwell on them now, but we can talk about them after I've relieved my conscience by confessing that I had another motive besides our old friendship for making this trip and stopping to see you."

"I can't imagine what such a reason would be," Jessie said calmly when her friend fell silent. "But go on, tell me."

"Arthur was a very wealthy man. I lived in a world of ease and luxury that I'd known existed, but never had any hope of entering. But shortly after his death, the estate he'd left began dwindling."

"And you didn't know the reason?"

"Oh, I knew the reason, Jessie. Most of his income was in dividends from a gold mine in Arizona. Suddenly the dividends began getting smaller and smaller. Now they've almost completely stopped. And I'm sure that there's some kind of dishonesty involved on the part of the head of the company." Lucy was silent for a moment, then in a sudden rush of words, she added, "Jessie, the other reason I've come to see you is to ask your help in finding out what's happened to that gold mine and why, and what I should do about it."

For a moment after listening to Lucy Chalmers's story, Jessie sat silent. Then she said, "Gold mines do stop producing ore sometimes, Lucy. If a vein runs out, there just isn't any more gold to dig. Are you sure that's not what's happened to the one your husband's money was coming from?"

"I suppose it's possible," Lucy replied. "But Arthur's attorney—who was a very good friend of his, and of mine, too, after our marriage—said he had a feeling that something odd was going on at the mine, and that I should investigate."

"Did he suggest what that odd something might've been?"

"No. He wrote to an attorney in Arizona asking him to look into the mine's operation. After two or three months, he finally got an answer. The Arizona lawyer hinted that he wasn't satisfied he'd gotten a true picture of the situation from the manager of the mine, but said that he couldn't put his finger on anything definite. He just came away with an impression that more investigation might be necessary."

"Did he offer to do the investigating?"

Lucy shook her head. "That's one of the reasons I believed his letter. He didn't even hint that I ought to retain him to look into the mine's operation. He said right out that he wasn't an expert in gold mining and suggested that I should find someone who was."

"It sounds like he was being honest," Jessie agreed.

"Yes, his letter impressed me that way, too. And then I thought of you, Jessie. I remembered that your father had left you some gold mines, and as smart a pupil as you were, and with Arizona being so close to Texas, I was just sure that you'd know who could help me."

"I'm not what you'd call an expert on gold mining, Lucy," Jessie protested. "But I have had to learn a little bit about them, because Alex had some substantial mining interests which I inherited. Exactly where in Arizona is this mine located?"

"It's outside a town up in the northern part, a place called Prescott. It's the capital of Arizona Territory, so it must be a city of some size."

"I don't think you'll find many cities in Arizona Territory that resemble those you're familiar with," Jessie said. "And as for Arizona being close to Texas—well, it's quite a distance, Lucy."

44

"But, Jessie, when I looked at the map to find it, I couldn't help noticing how close it is!"

Jessie did not reply at once. Then she said, "I'm sure you've talked with Steven about this. After all, it's part of his inheritance, too. What does he say?"

"Making this trip West was his idea. When the mine stock dividends finally dwindled to nothing, he suggested that we ought to find out for ourselves what was wrong."

"Shouldn't he be in here with us, then?"

Lucy shook her head. "Not tonight, Jessie. It was also his idea that I have a private talk with you first."

Jessie stood up and went to the bookcase wall. She selected an atlas from its well-stocked shelves and opened it. She thumbed through it until she'd found the map she was looking for, and then placed the big book on the desk.

"Come look at this with me," she invited Lucy. "I don't think you or Steven have studied maps very much."

"I don't suppose we've studied them; I know I haven't. If you'll remember, I taught English and deportment at the Academy, not geography."

"I remember quite well." Jessie smiled as her guest came across the room to join her at the desk. "But you can't have forgotten all the geography you must've studied at some time when you were going to school yourself."

"Goodness, Jessie! That was a long time ago, when I was a great deal closer to your age than to my own."

Jessie had opened the atlas to a page which showed the North American continent on a linear scale instead of the more familiar Mercator version. On this scale, with its polyconic projection, the northern portion of the continent showed how much wider the land area was at the south. The northeastern sector of the United States now appeared in its true dimension, shrunken when compared to the wide spread of the southwestern states and territories.

"My goodness!" Lucy exclaimed. "Why, I never realized before how tiny the states in the East are compared to the West! Gracious, Jessie! All of New England looks like a little hen-yard! It seems to shrink up compared to the way Texas and New Mexico and Arizona and Nevada Territories spread out on this map!"

"Alex showed me this," Jessie said, "and told me that when he got involved in ocean shipping as a young man one of the first things he'd learned was that the world really is round, and that when you look at it on a flattened-out map you get a false impression of distances and areas."

"Well, I can see now that it's a great deal farther to Arizona than I'd thought it would be when we got to Texas. No wonder it seemed like such a long trip here from New Orleans!"

"It is a long trip," Jessie agreed. "But neither Ki nor I will mind that."

Lucy stood in silence for a long moment, her face very thoughtful. At last she said, "Jessie, I don't have any right to expect you to go with Steven and me to find out about that gold mine. Neither of us realized what I was asking you to do when we talked about it. But now I see what an imposition—"

"Don't worry a bit about that," Jessie replied. "I remember how wonderful you were in helping me when I got the news that Alex had been killed. You treated me just as my mother would've done if she'd lived. I owe you a great deal more than you owe me, Lucy."

"You really think there's something wrong at the mine?"

"From what you've told me, there's a pretty good chance that something crooked is going on. I've been around enough mines to know what to look for, and Ki knows as much about mining as I do, perhaps more. Between us, we should be able to find out what's happening. Even if there's no crooked work going on, you won't feel right about your situation until you know exactly what the facts are."

"But it's so much longer a trip than I'd realized, Jessie. I still don't feel right—"

"And I wouldn't feel right if I didn't go with you," Jessie told her firmly. "Let's just consider it settled and say no more about it."

"But such a long trip—"

"Not very long. It'll only take us about as long as it did for you to get here from New Orleans."

"Four days, almost five?"

"About that." Jessie studied the atlas, which still lay open on the desk beside them. "We'll have to take the I&GN from here to El Paso, where we can connect with the new line the Santa Fe's building to California. And the Santa Fe's already started on a spur road up to the Grand Canyon; it'll almost certainly go through Prescott, since that's the territorial capital."

"How do you know so much about railroads, Jessie?" Lucy frowned. "Goodness! It seems to me that you must either ride the train a lot or else you've got a map in your brain."

"Looking after all the business interests that I inherited from Alex has meant that Ki and I do quite a bit of traveling," Jessie explained.

"Of course. I hadn't thought of that."

"We'd better stay here so that you can rest for a few days, though," Jessie went on. "The delay won't have any effect on whatever's happening to the gold mine, and I'm sure that you and Steven would like to get a look at the ranch."

"Of course we would. I know that Steven's really been looking forward to seeing the Circle Star."

"It's settled, then," Jessie said. "We'll stay here long enough for both of you to look around and rest after your trip from New Orleans. Then we'll go to Arizona."

Chapter 5

"I'm really glad you decided to go to the mine with Mother and me, Jessie," Steven Chalmers said.

He and Jessie were sitting beside a stockpond, finishing their lunch. Sun and the utility horse that Jessie had chosen for Steven to ride were tethered on the other side of the little spring-fed pool, cropping the drying grass. Steven was sitting beside her, his long legs stretched in front of him, encased in knee-high Eastern-style riding boots and flared saddle trousers. Jessie had not put on her jeans for their ride on such a warm, sunny day. She wore a thin blouse and a riding skirt.

Steven went on. "Mother's been worrying about those mining shares for the past several months. Anything we learn about the mine when we go to Arizona is going to relieve her mind, whether it's good news or bad."

"I hope she understands that it could be either," Jessie told him. "Any kind of a mine can come to the end of its main vein, and just stop producing overnight."

"I'm not sure she does understand," Steven went on thoughtfully. "Or maybe she does, and won't admit that the mine could simply have run out of ore."

"Well, for your sake as well as hers, I hope that whatever we find is good news," Jessie told him. "I can tell from what Lucy's said that it'd be a real blow to both of you if the mine should have petered out."

"It wouldn't be the blow to me that it would be to her," Steven said. "The idea that I'd have to go to work doesn't bother me, but the trouble is I've never had to work. I'm not sure I could find a job that would support both of us, and I certainly couldn't hope to find one that would allow us to keep living in the style we have now."

"If you should need a job, you might let me know," Jessie suggested. "As you know, I inherited Alex's business interests, and they were pretty widespread. I'm sure there are always openings somewhere."

Steven hesitated for a moment, then looked at Jessie and said quietly, "I appreciate your offer, Jessie, but I don't think you'll be hearing from me, even if the mine happens to be worthless now. If I came to you for a job, I'd always have a feeling that I'd be living on charity, not doing an honest day's work for an honest wage. I don't think I could respect myself if I did that."

Jessie looked at her companion with new eyes. The ride they were taking was really the first time they'd exchanged more than a few casual remarks, or been together away from others. Steven and Ki had arranged to go out together on a day's tour of the Circle Star, but Ed Wright had come to the main house before breakfast to enlist Ki's tracking skill in running to earth a panther that one of the cowhands had reported killing steers in the broken, gullied area that lay on the eastern side of the ranch.

Rather than disappoint her guest, Jessie had volunteered to take Ki's place. During their ride, Jessie had been kept busy answering the young New Englander's questions about the ranch. He'd shown a lively interest in everything from the differences between cattle breeds and the qualities ranchers looked for in cow-ponies to the different kinds of soil and vegetation they'd encountered.

At the beginning of their ride, Steven was still marveling at the size of the ranch, and Jessie'd tried to explain the economics of ranching in a semi-arid region, where unusually large areas of grazing land were required to sustain a cattle herd. After they'd ridden a few miles from the main house she'd begun veering their course southward in order to make her point, the south range being the most arid of the Circle Star's vast expanse.

She'd expected to find cattle on the range they were riding over, for the waterhole where they'd stopped for lunch was the only one within several miles. Though Steven had kept scanning the sun-parched, rolling rangeland, the only steers they'd seen had been a few scattered animals in the distance, and he hadn't seemed to understand when Jessie had tried to explain that the steers clustered into herds only on range where there was plenty of both graze and water. Now, their lunch finished, Jessie glanced at the sky and scrambled quickly to her feet.

"We'd better think about riding back toward the house," she said. "We've been so busy talking that I haven't been watching the sky, and from the looks of that line of clouds on the horizon, there might be a rainstorm coming this way."

Steven looked up. The sky directly overhead was cloudless and clear, and the clouds to the south and west were almost invisible, a thin line of gray on the distant horizon. He said, "Why, those clouds are a long way off, Jessie.

51

They won't get here for three or four hours."

"Clouds in this country can move a lot faster than you think," she replied.

"But I was hoping we'd ride on to that line shack you said you'd show me. I've never seen one, and hearing you talk about them yesterday has made me really curious to look at it."

Jessie glanced up again, and even to her weather-wise eyes the cloudbank seemed to be hanging almost motionless on the far horizon.

"All right," she said. "We'll go on to the line shack. If the rain gets here before we get back to the main house we might get wet, but I don't suppose that being caught in a shower would be a new experience for you, living where you do."

"No. The one thing we can be sure of at home is that it's going to rain sooner rather than later."

"I suppose you could say that about any place." Jessie smiled. "But here on the prairie the rain almost always seems to get here later."

She glanced at the clouds again. Even during the short time that had passed since they'd left the waterhole, what had been a finger-thin line of light gray had become a fast-rising bank of puffy, bluish gray, almost black, its movement clearly visible as it swept toward them. Now and then the blackness was broken by the brilliant zigzag flashes of lightning bolts, each flash followed by a sharp clap of thunder.

"We'd better hurry to that line shack," Jessie went on. "That's not just a light shower, it's a big thunderstorm."

"I'm sure you've gotten caught in the rain before, and I know I have." Steven smiled. "The worst that can happen to us is that we'll get wet."

"In this country, getting wet isn't the problem," Jessie

said. "There's lightning in that storm, and a lightning bolt's always drawn to the highest object in its path."

"Yes, I know. When a storm blows in back home, the tall trees really suffer."

"Out here where there aren't any trees, the bolt will run along the barbwire if there's a fence anywhere near. In this flat prairie country we're in now there aren't any fences between us and the Circle Star's boundary fence. We're the highest things around, Steven."

"You sound really concerned," he frowned.

"I am. A couple of years ago I saw what one of our Circle Star hands looked like when he'd been struck and killed by a lightning bolt on this south range, and it wasn't very pretty. Let's speed up."

Suiting her action to her words, Jessie nudged Sun's flank with her bootheel. The big palomino picked up its pace, and when Steven realized that Jessie was deadly serious, he dug his heels into the sides of his own mount.

They raced across the barren prairie for perhaps a quarter of an hour, Jessie watching the sky, a worried frown gathering on her face as the line of black clouds moved toward them with increasing speed. Around them, the rolling prairie was darkened when the clouds hid the sun, and suddenly the air was chilled. As the storm continued to advance, more lightning bolts stabbed through the blackened sky, and the sharp explosions that followed their brilliant flashes came nearer as well as closer together.

Occasional big raindrops began to splatter, hitting the dry shortgrass prairie soil with liquid thunks that sounded like small spent bullets. By the time they could see the line shack ahead, the rain was pelting them in small, sporadic bursts that lasted only a few minutes at a time, but were heavy enough to dampen their clothing. The true front of the storm was so close to them now that they could see the rain it carried descending in what appeared to be a single sheet of water below the jagged clouds. Now and then thunder roared as a lightning bolt shot its jagged brilliant zigzag line out of the clouds.

Jessie pointed to the shack and the silvery strands of the Circle Star's boundary fence just beyond it. The cabin was a small one, its board-and-batten sides unpainted, with a roof of corrugated iron sheeting that had been extended along one side to form a horse-shelter.

Steven nodded in response to Jessie's gesture and reined his horse to follow her to the cabin. She swung to the ground as she reached it and led Sun into the shelter of its extended eaves. Steven dismounted and led his pony in to follow hers. They stood beside the horses for a moment, watching the storm line's steady advance. By now the rain line had reached the line shack, and its pelting drops were drumming on its tin roof.

"We might as well go inside," Jessie said. "There's no way of predicting what this storm will do. The rain may last for only a few minutes, or it might pour an hour or two. I've seen some storms like this that lasted all night, and we're in the only place within eight or ten miles that will give us and the horses any shelter. It's easy to see that we're going to have to stay here until this blow passes over."

"Suppose one of those lightning bolts hits that metal roof?" Steven asked.

"Maybe you didn't see the lightning-rod. I had them put on all our line shacks after that hand I told you about got killed."

"I guess you have a door key?"

"We don't lock the line shacks, Steven. There's nothing in them that a stranger passing by would consider worth stealing, and now and then a hand from our neighbor's spread uses one when he gets caught like we are now."

Steven followed Jessie as she hurried around the shack's corner and went inside. He blinked for a moment in the dimmed light that trickled through the single small window, set high in the back wall behind a little monkey stove. A couple of bare shelves were attached to the wall beside the window, narrow bunks with thin mattresses in blue and white striped ticking filled one wall, while a small square table and two chairs stood against the opposite wall.

Steven smiled. "This is sort of a bare-bones place."

"All line shacks are," Jessie assured him. "They're not used very often, you see."

"At least we'll be able to stay dry in here." Steven fought the shiver that rippled through him in the cold air and went on. "But a fire in that stove would sure be welcome."

"Welcome but impossible, I'm afraid. When one of the men comes here to stay a day or two, he brings whatever wood he needs. I didn't take time to put a blanket-roll on Sun's saddle, because it was so clear and warm when we started from the house, and I didn't think we'd need any coats. Big rainstorms don't hit very often at this time of the year, but when they do they chill the air very fast."

"I can see now that you weren't just spinning a yarn when you were telling us about Texas weather last night," Steven went on. "I thought it was just a sort of joking story that you save to amuse strangers."

"I leave telling Texas stories to the hands, Steven." Jessie smiled. Then her face grew serious and she went on. "I do know the only way for us to be a little bit more comfortable in here is to sit down on one of those cots and huddle as close together as we can get. That way, we'll keep each other warm."

"Let's do it, then," he agreed.

Steven stepped over to the nearest cot and settled down. Jessie did not hesitate, but followed him at once and sat beside him. He looked around at her, his eyebrows rising in an unspoken question.

"Go ahead," she said. "Put your arms around me and I'll put mine around you and we'll squeeze as close together as we can possibly get."

Steven's hesitation vanished. He took Jessie in his arms and pulled her to him. She wasted no time in embracing him, and as they clung together in the increasingly gelid air, their bodies began to grow warmer. They'd been sitting in their embrace for perhaps a quarter of an hour before either spoke.

"It's a shame that there isn't enough room in here for us to keep warm by doing some exercising," Steven remarked after they'd squeezed together for a few minutes. "My legs are cold."

"So are mine," Jessie told him. Then she went on, "It's even worse that we don't have any kind of cover. It's getting colder, and if we had some sort of cover we could both snuggle down under it and get really warm. As it is, I think we'd better do the next-best thing."

"What's that?"

"We'll lie down and cuddle up instead of just sitting here and letting our legs and feet freeze." As she spoke, Jessie shrugged out of Steven's embrace. She lay down on her side, facing him. He'd gotten to his feet and stood looking down at her. Jessie said, "Come on, Steven. We'll be a lot warmer."

"I'm sure we will," he replied, and lay down on the narrow bunk beside her.

Jessie turned to lie on her side. Steven was stretched out now, and she pushed her body against him. He hesitated for a moment, then put his arms around her and pulled her

56

close to him, spooning his thighs and legs against hers. They lay without moving for several minutes, and Jessie was just beginning to feel warm again when she felt an unmistakable pressure against her buttocks and realized that Steven was well on the way to an erection.

She made no comment, but lay motionless as she felt the bulge of his shaft continue to swell and grow firmer. Steven was silent, too. Then Jessie felt a breath of cool air flooding the crevice between them as he moved gently away and disengaged the close contact of their bodies.

For several months before she and Ki had made their trip to Austin, Jessie had been content. She'd had a vague idea that during their journey she might run into a man who'd make a suitable bed partner, but had been too busy to seek one out. And in the busy routine of their short stay she had not encountered one to whom she'd been attracted before they had returned to the Circle Star.

Now, in her intimate embrace with Steven, she felt a sudden pulsing of long-suppressed need. A moment of thought convinced her that under the circumstances the stepson of her former teacher would not be likely to take the lead in making an advance, and she decided quickly that it was up to her to be the instigator. She pressed backward and restored their former close contact. When she pushed herself firmly against Steven's crotch she felt his body grow tense.

"I liked the feeling of you pushing against me," she said softly.

Steven lay silent for a long moment. When he did speak, he said, "So did I. But I didn't want to make you angry."

"Do I sound like I'm angry?"

"No, but—" He cut off his words.

"We're not children, Steven."

"Right now, I feel like a gawky kid, not being able to keep from—" He stopped short again.

"Suppose I told you that I liked what I was feeling?"

Steven hesitated only a few seconds before asking, "Did you?"

"Very much indeed. And if you want me to prove it . . ." While she was speaking, Jessie slipped her hand between their bodies. When she'd found the bulge in Steven's crotch she closed her fingers as best she could over his still-bulging erection.

"Are you suggesting what I think you are? Do you want me to go ahead, or are you just teasing me?" he asked. His voice betrayed his surprise.

"Whatever I am, I'm not a tease." By now Jessie was unbuttoning Steven's fly.

"No. You're just a lot more direct than I'd ever dreamed you'd be, Jessie. Can you get out of your skirt, lying down this way?"

"Not easily or quickly, but I'll manage to be ready when you are."

As she spoke, Jessie was removing her hand from Steven's crotch to unbutton the side placquet of her divided skirt. She could feel Steven moving behind her, and quickly slid the skirt and her underpants down her thighs, then arched her back to bring her bare buttocks closer to him. Impatient with the delay, she groped for his erection, encountered his hands and brushed them aside, found his pulsing shaft and positioned it.

"Now!" she said. "Drive into me!"

Steven obeyed. Jessie gasped as she felt his shaft penetrate her fully with his initial lunge. Then he began a fast triphammer driving that set her squirming and soon had her quivering eagerly as she rushed to an unexpectedly sudden climax.

She pulsed with quivering delight for a long, drawn-out moment, then as Steven showed no sign of stopping, Jessie arched her back to allow him to thrust even more deeply. He continued his slow, measured plunges, and she locked her arms around his chest and began arching her back, lifting her hips to meet them with upthrust hips while she waited for the onset of another rippling spasm.

After several minutes, Steven began shuddering and she gasped, "Not yet, Steven, not yet! I'm enjoying myself too much to want it to end too quickly!"

"So am I!" he told her. He slowed the measured tempo of his deep drives, and at the end of a thrust he let himself down until he was resting on Jessie's quivering form. "Let's just rest quietly for a few minutes. I don't want this to end for a long time myself."

Jessie offered him her lips, and Steven met them in a protracted, tongue-entwining kiss that they held until both were breathless. His hands sought Jessie's full, firm breasts, and he caressed them gently, first with his stroking fingers, then with his lips and tongue, until Jessie began quivering again.

When Steven sought her lips again, she met his kiss gladly, and he held the caress until she began quivering once more.

Breaking their kiss, Jessie said, "I'm ready again now, if you are. Start whenever you want to."

Once more Steven began his long steady plunges, setting a slower tempo now that their first dammed-up passion had been drained. After the earlier release of her long pent-up needs, Jessie responded more slowly, and this time she made no effort to hold back her mounting response. When Steven began to speed his long thrusts, she responded quickly. They mounted the slope of rising passion together and reached its peak once more, then shuddered through their fulfillment and lay supine until the ebb.

As she lay with Steven's body resting on hers, Jessie realized for the first time that the driving rain was no longer drumming on the line shack's tin roof. She said, "It's a long ride to the main house, Steven. We'd better start back if we want to get there before dark."

"I'd just as soon stay here," he said. "But if you should hear a little tapping on your door tonight, will you let me in?"

"You know I will," she told him. "Tonight and for as many nights as we stay here. And don't forget, we'll be together for quite a while on our trip, too."

"That's what I'm thinking of now," he replied as he bent to kiss her. "And I'm glad Arizona's such a long way from here. It'll give us that much more time to spend together."

★

Chapter 6

"Until we started up these mountains, I'd thought Arizona Territory was just one big stretch of sandy desert," Lucy Chalmers remarked as she gazed out the window of the passenger coach.

There was little to hold the attention of a traveler in the land through which the train was now chugging. The tracks wound along the western slope of a ragged line of low-rising mountains, their sides for the most part only barren stretches of coarse ocher soil broken by the skeleton-white shelf of a limestone outcrop, and an occasional ragged cluster of low-topped scrub pine trees.

Everywhere along the right-of-way there were signs of the railroad's recent construction. Where there had once been a gandydancer camp there were the broken wheels of wagons, tangles of discarded harness, and scraps of clothing faded by the sun and tattered by the wind. Occasionally, away from the road, the scruffy, shrunken carcass of a dead mule or horse could be seen, its hide peeling away in big patches to disclose the white bones of ribs and spine and skull.

"This still looks better to me than the desert land we came through further south," Steven commented. "And I'm beginning to think I might enjoy it here more than back home. At least it's not hemmed in by houses and people crammed into tiny bits of land." Turning to Jessie, who was sitting opposite him, beside Lucy, he asked, "What's this town we're going to like?"

"I haven't any idea, Steven," she replied. "I've never been there before. But I imagine it'll be pretty much the same as some of the larger towns we've passed through. It should be a fair-sized place, since it's the territorial capital."

"Well, at last we're finally getting there," Steven went on. "I didn't have any idea that it'd take us almost a week to get here. I had the same idea Mother had, that after we got on the train we'd just have a few hours to travel."

Ahead of them the whistle shrilled, and the train began to slow down. They peered out the window, but could see no signs of a town ahead. Ki came down the aisle and settled into the vacant seat beside Steven.

"Ten or fifteen minutes more and we'll be there," he told them. "The men in the baggage car are already stacking suitcases to unload, and I've made sure that none of our bags will be left on the train when we stop at Prescott."

Even before Ki had finished speaking the train slowed down further, and a short time later the conductor came through the coach, calling the Prescott station-stop. The slow forward motion of the train quickly became a crawl. Then its brakes rasped roughly with a last despairing screech of iron brake-shoes on steel wheels.

Ten minutes later Jessie, Ki, Lucy, and Steven were

standing beside their piled-up luggage in front of the red brick Santa Fe depot. Even before Ki and Steven had finished piling the luggage on the brick sidewalk, a hackman had wheeled his vehicle around in the middle of the street and reined up in front of them.

"I guess you folks'll be needing a ride into town," he said. "And if you're looking for a place to stay while you're here, you'll find that the Burke Hotel is the one all them big high-up muckety-mucks that's got business at the capital picks out. Be glad to take you there, and your bags, too. Two bits apiece for the four of you, and the Chink can get up here on the seat by me. You got so many suitcases, I'd say a dime apiece for them."

"That sounds reasonable." Jessie nodded. She glanced inquiringly at Lucy, who nodded agreement. She turned back to the cabbie. "Very well. And Ki will ride inside with us."

For a moment Jessie thought the hackman was going to object, but after a moment he said, "I don't guess he'd mind handing them suitcases up to me, would he? It'll take a lot less time to stow 'em on the rack if I don't have to get down and muscle 'em up myself."

Before Jessie could reply, Ki spoke up. "Of course. I'll be glad to." He tossed the party's half-dozen valises and suitcases up to the hackman while the others got into the carriage. Then he told the hackie, "I've changed my mind about riding inside. I'll get up and sit with you on the way to the hotel."

"Suit yourself," the cabbie replied. "As long as your boss don't blame me, I don't care where you ride."

"That's not the impression I got a moment ago," Ki told the hackie as he settled into the seat beside him. "Is it that the people in Prescott don't like Orientals?"

"Why, they ain't mad at nobody," the cabman said.

"Not as long as you chinks does your jobs and don't try to mix with folks that ain't your own kind."

Ki was not surprised at the man's reply. He'd heard the same thoughts expressed before, in other places, applied not only to Orientals, but to the Indians native to the land as well as to blacks and Mexicans. His expression did not change, nor did the tone of his voice, when he spoke again.

"I imagine there are places here where I can find others who came from the Orient?"

"I guess you mean Chinks," the driver replied. The cab was approaching a large, blocklike two-story building made of dark gray native granite, and the man pointed to it with his buggywhip. "That there's the territorial capital. Right on the other side of it's Whiskey Row; that's where—"

"I know," Ki broke in. "I've seen streets like it in other places. That's where the saloons and gambling-house are, and I suppose the red-light houses are close by, too."

"You called the card first turn," the hackie replied. "The girls are right behind the Row. And down a ways from it, on Granite Street, that's where you'll find the Chinese joints that ain't moved out to the Gardens yet."

Ki frowned as he asked, "The Gardens?"

"Sure. Chinese Gardens, that what they call the shanties the Chinks has built out in Miller's Valley. It ain't far from town—three, maybe four miles. Any time you wanta go out there, just come down to my stand by the depot, and I'll take you out. Cost you a half-dollar, though. It ain't like taking you someplace that's right in town."

"I'll remember," Ki promised.

While they'd been talking, the cabman had guided his horse around the wide expanse of fenced ground that enclosed the little hillock on which the territorial capital

64

stood, and he now reined the animal into a wide, brick-paved thoroughfare. It was lined with stores and commercial buildings. Only a few of them were of frame construction; the most popular building materials in Prescott were obviously red brick and granite blocks.

Ki went on, "I suppose this is the main business street?"

"That's right. Gurley Street. That's the Burke Hotel just a little ways ahead, that big three-story building."

"You've been very helpful," Ki told the man. "But I still need to ask a question or two."

"Ask away."

"I suppose there's a livery stable close to the hotel? Miss Starbuck will want to rent a buggy or a shay, and I'll probably need to rent a horse a time or two while we're here."

"Well, now." The hackman frowned. "I figure I can take anybody just about any place they'd wanta go, long as it ain't so far out from town that I'd lose a lot of fares."

"Oh, I'm sure you can," Ki replied. "But you'd be tied up waiting for us, and there might be times when Miss Starbuck and I would be going to different places. But I'm sure we can find a livery stable without too much trouble."

"I tell you what," the cabbie said. "You go out of the hotel when you need a horse or a rig, and go right down to the corner of Gurley Street and Montezuma. Turn down Montezuma and go just a little ways till you get to Riordan's Livery. Tell Jim Riordan that Sam sent you. I guarantee he'll treat you right."

"Thank you," Ki said as the hackie reined around in the center of the street and pulled up in front of the three-story building that bore the sign BURKE HOTEL. Ki took a pair of cartwheels out of his pocket and handed them to the cabman. "This should cover our ride and a bit more for the information."

Dropping off the seat, he opened the door and handed Jessie and Lucy Chalmers to the sidewalk.

"There wasn't time to ask the hackman where the gold mine is," he told Jessie. "But the hotel clerk will be able to tell us that. And I'm sure I have all the other information we'll need to allow us to get around."

"Good," Jessie nodded. "And if—"

She broke off when a brass-button-uniformed bellhop came out of the hotel and looked from Steven to Ki to Jessie to Lucy.

"Are you folks checking in?" he asked.

Jessie nodded. "Yes. If you'll take our bags to the desk, we'll be right there." Turning back to Ki, she went on, "The day's still young, Ki. We have most of the afternoon left, so there's plenty of time for us to start looking around and asking a few questions. From what Lucy told me on the train, I have a pretty good list of things I'd like to know about the Empire Mining Company. If the mine's not too far from town, I'd like to start by going out there."

"Do you want me to go with you?"

Jessie shook her head. "No. I think it'll be better if just Lucy and I go. You and Steve can make some discreet inquiries around town, though. Perfectly innocent ones, of course."

Ki nodded. "I have an idea that I might be able to get some even more useful information tonight, unless you have plans that include me. I found out from our cabman where the Oriental section of town is, and I'm sure that Prescott isn't any different from other places. People talk very freely, even when their servants are listening."

Ki spoke without rancor. A son of Japanese nobility himself, he'd long ago accepted the fact that Orientals in America were looked on generally as being useful primarily as house servants.

66

"Then you explore your field, and I'll look into mine," Jessie said as they followed the bellman into the hotel. "We'll compare notes this evening, of course."

"I hope you won't hesitate to speak up if I start to say something I shouldn't, Jessie," Lucy said as they crossed the rattling boards of a wide bridge that spanned a large creek.

A short distance beyond the bridge, Jessie reined the horse to a halt in front of a barely visible side road. Sparse grass and scrawny weeds almost concealed the deep ruts made by the wheels of many heavily laden wagons. On one side of the road, barely visible, a sign read EMPIRE MINE CO. The words had been burned into a narrow slab of wood sawed at one end into a point. Jessie pointed to it.

"I'd say we've found what we're looking for," she said as she reined the horse into the side road.

"Are you sure?" Lucy frowned as the buggy lurched and swayed over the rutted trace. "It doesn't look like anybody's used this road for years."

"Months, perhaps. You'll see the wide ruts that ore-wagons make, if you look closely," Jessie told her. "But there's no indication of how far it is to the mine."

"It can't be very far, from what the man at the hotel told us. But I don't mind telling you, Jessie, that the closer we get to asking questions of the mining company manager, the more nervous and shaky I feel. I won't know whether or not I'll be getting truthful answers."

"Don't worry," Jessie assured her former teacher. "I won't let you be fooled by anything you're told that I feel sounds suspicious. But remember what I mentioned back at the Circle Star. Gold mines—or any other mines, for that matter—can't always go on producing ore forever."

"Oh, I remember that quite well," Lucy assured her.

67

"And I'll do my best not to make any foolish mistakes."

"I'm sure you will."

Lucy made no further comment, and Jessie concentrated on keeping the buggy from lurching and bouncing too badly on the rutted road. It was a typical mining road, its surface deeply scored by the wide wheels of ore-wagons, and clodded with lumps of stone-hard soil which had dropped from the big hooves of the huge draft horses that pulled them.

When the buggy had covered the first few hundred yards after turning off, Jessie's experience with similar roads that she'd used to travel to other mines had convinced her that there'd been no loaded ore-wagons on it for a long time. She turned to Lucy and remarked, "It looks as though your man at the mine was telling you the truth about one thing. The mine's certainly not moving any ore to a smelter, and hasn't been for quite some time."

"What makes you say that?" Lucy frowned. "We haven't even seen any sign of the mine yet."

"No, but this road tells its own story," Jessie replied, pointing to the ruts winding through the trees ahead of them. "Look at it closely, Lucy, and you'll see grass is sprouting in the deep wheel-ruts and hoofprints that catch and hold water. There aren't any fresh, deep wheel-ruts such as an ore-wagon would leave. If it were being used regularly by a large number of wagons, there'd be a lot more fresh horse-droppings than we've seen so far."

"I'd never have thought about looking for things like that," Lucy told Jessie after she'd studied the road a few moments. "I'm gladder than ever that you agreed to come here with me. Mr. Manfield may have been telling me the truth, then."

Jessie nodded. "There's always that possibility. But don't take what I've said as gospel. We ought to know a great deal more after we've actually seen the mine."

They saw the mine's buildings very soon. To Jessie, the scene was commonplace. There was a large, red-painted office building that had a ragged-edged sign, EMPIRE MINE CO., on its board-and-batten wall. A short distance away stood a truncated little shelter which rose above the shaft and gave access to the underground workings. Scattered over the half-acre clearing were the toolsheds and black-smith's shop, and the stacks of raw shoring timbers were very much like those which Jessie had seen at other mines.

To Lucy, the scene was new and fascinating. She pep-pered Jessie with questions during the few minutes re-quired to reach the office building and rein in beside it. Then, when Jessie had pulled up the horse and they were ready to dismount, Lucy's face grew soberly concerned.

"You're going to have to do most of the talking," she reminded Jessie unnecessarily. "Because in spite of every-thing you've explained to me, I'm afraid I might forget exactly what to say or what questions to ask."

"That's what I came along for, Lucy," Jessie replied. "Now get that panicked look off your face and let's go in and see what we can find out."

Although there were a half-dozen desks behind the railed enclosure that stood beyond the entrance door, only one of them was occupied. An elderly man wearing a green eyeshade was working at it, a massive ledger open in front of him. He looked up when Jessie and Lucy entered, then stood up and came to the divided rail.

"Yes, ladies?" he said. "What can I do for you?"

"I'm Mrs. Chalmers," Lucy replied. "From Holyoke, Massachussets. This is Miss Jessica Starbuck. I'm one of the stockholders in this mine, and if Mr. Manfield is here my friend and I would like to talk to him for a few min-utes."

For a moment the clerk stood impassively, studying Lucy and Jessie, then he nodded. "Mr. Manfield's in his office. I'm sure he's not too busy to see you, but I'll have to enquire."

When the clerk had tapped at the office door and disappeared inside, Lucy asked Jessie, her voice a worried whisper, "What if he doesn't agree to see us?"

"Then we'll make an appointment and come back tomorrow. And if we have to wait a week to see him and come back every day, that's what we'll do. But I have a feeling that even if he's not too pleased to see us, he won't refuse. Now, stop worrying, Lucy, and remember what we've talked about when we get into his office."

Jessie had hardly finished when the clerk and another man came through the office door. During the few moments needed for them to cross to the railing, Jessie sized up the mining company president with a few quick flicks of her eyes.

Manfield was a short man, compact of build. Despite the isolation of the mine's headquarters, he wore the subdued gray three-piece suit that was almost obligatory garb for executives in large cities. His dark hair showed some graying at the temples, and was swept back in a center part. He was clean-shaven, and his features had no attributes that would set him apart in a crowd. He smiled as he approached the railing.

"Mrs. Chalmers?" he asked, looking from Lucy to Jessie.

"I'm Lucinda Chalmers," Lucy replied. "And this is my friend, Miss Starbuck."

"I'm very pleased to meet both of you charming ladies," the mine manager said. He opened the gate in the railing and went on with a half-bow, "If you'd like to step into my office, we can have our chat in private."

As he stood aside to let Jessie and Lucy pass, Manfield went on. "I hope you'll pardon my curiosity, but are you the late Alex Starbuck's daughter, Miss Jessica?"

"Yes, I am," Jessie nodded.

"Although I never had the honor of meeting your father, I've naturally heard both your names," Manfield went on as they walked across the outer office. "His death was a great loss not only to the United States, but to the business community, and I'm sure a much greater loss to you."

"Of course," Jessie replied. "No one can ever fill his place."

Inside his office, Manfield closed the door and pulled two chairs up to the massive flat-topped desk that dominated the room. He waited until Jessie and Lucy were seated, then went to his own high-backed upholstered chair and settled into it.

"I think that I know the reason for your visit, Mrs. Chalmers," he began. "You're not the only company stockholder who's concerned about the condition of the Titan, but I believe you've traveled the greatest distance to inquire about it."

When Manfield showed no signs of continuing, Lucy said, "My late husband's main income was the dividends from his mine stock, Mr. Manfield. Now my stepson and I depend on it. I must know when the dividend payments will be made again."

"Can we put that question aside for a moment?" Manfield asked. "I'd like you to allow me to tell you first why we've been forced to suspend the dividend payments."

"I think the letter I got from you explained that," Lucy told him. "The mine ran out of gold."

"I suppose you can phrase it that way." He nodded. "But it's not quite the most accurate description of what happened."

71

"Then give me a more accurate one, if you don't mind," Lucy said after she'd glanced covertly at Jessie and gotten an encouraging nod in response.

Manfield frowned as he replied. "To be quite precise, the large vein of ore that's been so productive for so many years suddenly ended at an underground earth fault. At some time in the past—nobody knows when, of course—there was a huge earthquake that pushed a wall of underground granite across the vein of gold. That's what all the geologists we've brought in for consultation tell us has happened."

When the mine manager paused, Jessie looked at Lucy, wondering if she was going to ask the question she'd suggested if the word "geologist" was mentioned. When Lucy did not speak, Jessie did, just as Manfield opened his mouth to continue.

"I suppose you brought in geologists who are quite familiar with this goldfield?" she asked. "And who aren't employed by this company or any competitive company on a regular basis?"

"You may be sure we did, Miss Starbuck," Manfield answered quickly. "But we didn't stop with geologists' opinions. Since the miners suddenly ran into that wall of solid rock, we've kept a crew of them hard at work digging exploratory shafts in all directions, down and up and on both sides, trying to find the vein again. So far, they haven't been able to."

"You're not going to give up trying, are you?" Lucy asked, struggling to keep her voice from showing her anxiety.

"Certainly not. But there's a limit to how far we can carry our explorations. We've spent all our reserve funds and just about exhausted our credit."

"What's going to happen to my dividends if you don't

find the vein again?" Lucy asked, fighting to keep her voice from trembling.

"I'm afraid we'll have to liquidate the company," Manfield told her. "If we do that, of course, there'll be no more dividends, for you or for anyone else."

Chapter 7

For a moment after Manfield made his statement, Jessie and Lucy sat staring at him. Then Jessie asked, "Mr. Manfield, instead of tunneling around the rock wall that's blocking the vein, have you thought of sinking a new shaft beyond the granite formation?"

"That was the first thing we thought of, Miss Starbuck. But while we're reasonably sure the gold vein continues on the other side of the granite formation, we can't be absolutely positive. We decided against the idea because of the cost of sinking a new main shaft and moving the hoists and other equipment would simply have been too great."

"And I suppose the company's reserves are running low?"

"Of course." Manfield nodded. "There's never been any secret about that. If they weren't, Mrs. Chalmers and the other stockholders would still be receiving their dividends."

"Then you don't think there's much chance of finding where the gold vein is on the other side of the granite?" Lucy asked.

"Now, I didn't say that, Mrs. Chalmers," Manfield said quickly. "All of us who're familiar with geology know that a vein of gold very seldom just disappears. It may diminish bit by bit and finally run out, but that isn't what's happening here at the Empire. The gold vein simply must continue somewhere behind that rock formation, and when we find it the mine will be just as rich as it ever was."

"Then all we can do is wait?" Lucy frowned.

"I'm afraid so," Manfield told her. "I'm sure we'll pick up the vein again when we've tunneled around the granite."

Jessie had been thinking about Manfield's explanation while he and Lucy talked. Now she said, "While we're here, I'd like to take a look at your underground work, Mr. Manfield. I don't suppose you'd have any objection?"

For a moment Manfield was silent. Then he said, "I don't have any, Miss Starbuck, but I'm afraid the miners would. As I'm sure you know, they have a superstition that it's bad luck for a woman to go underground where they're working."

"I've never heard that before, and I've been underground in several of the mines I own."

"In which the miners were natives of our own country, I would imagine?"

"Yes." Then a puzzled frown formed on her face and she asked, "Why should that matter?"

"Because our miners are about equally divided between Chinese and Boers who've emigrated from South Africa, the Transvaal. It's a very troubled country right now. In fact, England may have to send troops there to quiet the unrest. But they brought with them that superstition that a woman underground in a mine is bad luck, Miss Starbuck, and I'm afraid they'd walk off their jobs if you even entered the mine at its mouth."

Jessie replied thoughtfully, "Then I suppose I'll have to ask Ki to be my eyes. But he's more familiar with mining operations than I am. He was with my father for many years."

Manfield did not reply at once. Finally he said, "I don't have any objections, of course. But it's late in the day; the men will be leaving the shafts in another hour or so. Would tomorrow or the next day be soon enough?"

"Of course. We're stopping at the Burke Hotel; just leave word there if we don't happen to be in our rooms," Jessie said. Standing up, she turned to Lucy and went on, "I think we've taken up enough of Mr. Manfield's time. Suppose we go now and come back with Ki when he looks at the mine."

"You've mentioned Ki twice now, Miss Starbuck," Manfield said, frowning. "I assume it's someone's name?"

"Yes." Jessie nodded as they started toward the door. "Ki was my father's trusted assistant, and is now mine. He's as familiar with mining as most engineers."

"I see," the mine superintendent said. "When do you plan to return, then?"

"Tomorrow, perhaps?" Jessie suggested.

Manfield was silent for a moment, then he asked. "Would you be inconvenienced if I asked you to postpone your visit for a day or two?"

"Of course not. The day after tomorrow would be just as satisfactory."

"I'll look for you then," Manfield told her, opening the door for them. He faced Lucy and went on, "Now, I hope that I've answered all your questions satisfactorily, Mrs. Chalmers. I'll look forward to greeting you and Miss Starbuck when you return. You will be with her, I suppose?"

Before Lucy could reply, Jessie answered for her. "Of course. We'll be here early, so that Ki won't be rushed for time when he examines the underground work."

In the buggy, as they started back toward Prescott, Lucy said to Jessie, "Mr. Manfield seemed a bit upset when you told him that Ki was going into the mine to inspect it."

"Yes, he did," Jessie agreed. "Perhaps I'm being a bit too suspicious. But we've come a long way to find out what's wrong, so we'd better make the most thorough investigation we can while we're here."

"I'm so new to things of this sort that I don't really see what we can do," Lucy said. "What do you expect Ki to find?"

"If I had even a hint of that, Ki might not have to go underground and look at the mine shaft, Lucy. And while I might be looking for ghosts that don't even exist, perhaps it would be useful for me to go into the local bank and ask a few questions."

After watching Jessie and Lucy drive off toward the mine, Ki had not gone back into the hotel. He'd turned in the opposite direction and walked toward Prescott's most prominent landmark, the territorial capitol. When they'd passed the capitol earlier on the way from the depot he'd had only a glimpse of the imposing building.

As he approached it now, the capitol reminded him of some of the medieval castles he'd seen in Europe during his business trips there with Alex. Its gray granite-block walls rose three stories high over the little grassy knoll on which it stood. The high, slitlike windows at the tall, square turret that towered two stories above it somehow made the capitol seem out of place in Arizona Territory.

Ki did not go all the way to the capitol building, but

turned and strolled along Whiskey Row, glancing at the saloons and gambling parlors that lined the street. Even at this early hour of the afternoon, Whiskey Row had its share of drunks reeling from the saloons and disgruntled losers emerging from the halls of chance. He picked one of the losers rather than one of the drunks and stopped the man.

"I am a stranger here, sir," Ki said. "Can you direct me to Granite Street? I was told that there are restaurants there which serve oriental foods."

"Looking for some of your own kind, are you?" the man grunted. Then he turned to point. "Just go down that way till you come to Granite Street. You'll find what you're looking for there."

With a nod of thanks, Ki followed the man's directions; and when he turned the corner of Granite Street the signs in oriental ideographs as well as in English gave him the feeling that he'd suddenly been transported from Arizona Territory to a waterfront street in Shanghai or Fusan.

After his first quick glance Ki saw that the ideographs were all Chinese. Pushing aside his disappointment, he walked slowly along the deserted street until at last in the distance his eyes caught a sign in Japanese. He walked slowly along the almost deserted street until he could read the lettering. The English words at the top told him the establishment bore the name "The Peaceful Tea-House." Below it were the ideographs translating the name into Japanese, and under them, chopmarks which indicated that the building also housed a *do*. The combination of a tea-house and a martial-arts school was too great to resist. Ki opened the door and went inside.

There was no one in sight, either in the small entryway or in the larger room beyond it, where he could see tables dotting the floor. Then a door in the side wall of the entry opened and a man wearing a baggy white blouse and trousers stepped in. The blouse was secured at the waist by a narrow black sash. He looked at Ki, who had on his customary loose black trousers and jacket, the jacket secured by the black belt he'd earned so many years ago. When the man saw Ki's black belt his eyes widened.

Indicating the belt, he asked, *"Kobu-do?"*

Ki had not felt completely at home before, but he did now, as his countryman followed the old traditional method of greeting by asking for the name of the master who had bestowed the belt.

Although there were many who wore the coveted black belt, which signified mastery of the oriental martial arts, the traditions of *Kobu-do* were still alive. These stemmed from its beginning days, when the Manchus were setting out to conquer the offshore islands, and prohibited all inhabitants of the isles they had reduced to vassalage from carrying weapons.

This had marked the beginning of the art of combat without weapons, or at best with those which could be easily concealed, such as the *shuriken,* or those which could be improvised from the oar of a boat or a walking-staff, such as the *bo.* All training of the weaponless population had to be done secretly, and those skilled in these arts identified themselves by their sashes or belts. Now, several centuries later, some of the traditions of the ancient days, when *Kobu-do* was a hidden art, still survived.

Bending from the waist, Ki nodded and replied with the name of his first martial arts teacher. "Hirata Ki. It is in his honor that I have chosen to call myself Ki."

Bobbing a quick ceremonial bow at Ki's introduction, the newcomer responded in kind. "Chijin Yamatami," he said. "My *sensei* was Dinowan. Welcome to my humble *do.*"

"It is I who am honored to be here," Ki answered, matching the other man's bow. Neither Ki nor Chijin attempted to speak in Japanese. Because of the profusion of regional dialects common in the Orient, English had become the *lingua franca* of Asiatics who had found new homes in America.

"You do not need to seek a *do*," Chijin went on. "But you are welcome to mine. I was preparing tea when I heard you enter. You will join me, please?"

"Of course," Ki replied. "But I came only to talk."

"There is time. I have a pupil who will be here soon, but we need not hurry."

Turning, Chijin led Ki into the big bare room from which his restaurant had been formed by partitioning off a sizeable corner. In the alcove that the partition had left along one wall there was a charcoal brazier with a steaming kettle on it, a small table bearing tiny porcelain cups and a teapot, and several chairs. In common with most gymnasiums, the remainder of the space was furnished only by a half-dozen mats scattered over the polished floor.

Ki sat down while his impromptu host busied himself pouring boiling water from the kettle into the teapot. He carried the pot to the table and sat down across from Ki.

"You said you came to talk," Chijin told him. "I will listen while the tea steeps."

"I have come here with the lady whom I serve as I did her father before he died," Ki began. "His name was Alex Starbuck, and my debt of honor to him is great."

"I have heard the name Starbuck." Chijin nodded. "Among our people, it is an honored one."

"It is honored in this country as well," Ki replied. "But it is not on her business that we have made the trip. She has come to help a friend, who is also with us, as is her son. We have come to find out about the Empire Mining Company."

Again Chijin nodded. "I know of the mine, but I know nothing about it except that it brings up gold, and that it is a place where some of our people work. Most of the miners are Chinese, but there are some from our homeland."

Even the scrap of information that the mine employed Orientals was new to Ki. He looked at Chijin with renewed interest and asked, "Do you know many of these workmen?"

"A few."

"Do they come here to your tea-house?"

"Some do. And most of them live in the Gardens, where my humble home is located."

Ki frowned. "The Gardens?"

Chijin nodded. "We Orientals are not greatly liked here. The people of Prescott are not different from those elsewhere in America; they stay with their own kind and are more comfortable when people from other lands live away from them. Some years ago we Orientals began settling in a place close by. It is called Miller Valley, and is not far from town. The people in Prescott call it Chinese Gardens."

"Then that is where I should go to find out what I need," Ki said. "I had thought of trying to get a job at the mine so that I can meet the workers and talk with them, but it will be easier and take less time for me to go to their homes."

For a moment Chijin looked at Ki, his face puzzled. Then he asked, "Is whatever you and your employer are planning to do a secret, Ki?"

Ki framed his answer carefully. "I would like what I am

81

thinking of doing to draw no attention from the officials at the mine. That is all."

"Then you have come here to look into the trouble that they are having?"

"Perhaps you would not object to telling me first what you have heard of any trouble there," Ki suggested.

"All the workers know that the Empire mine has not sent any ore to the smelter for many months," Chijin replied.

"Do others know this also?"

"Everyone whispers about it, but no one can be sure. As the sage has said, 'the servants talk more freely when the master is away.'"

"What you have said is very interesting, and will be useful to Miss Starbuck," Ki told Chijin. "Perhaps you have heard some other whispers' as well. If you have, I would be in your debt if you would feel free to repeat them for me."

Chijin sipped his tea before replying. Then he told Ki, "I hear much gossip from my students. They are the sons of men who work at the Empire mine, and they discuss what they have heard their fathers tell their mothers. How much is true, I cannot say, but the men of our people who work at the mine no longer work together on the same vein."

"Some work elsewhere? Another shaft, another vein?"

"This is what I have heard. They have all been ordered not to talk about their work, even to one another. But they do talk to each other when they are here, or at home."

"If I might stay here a short time, and perhaps also return later to talk with some of these young men, I would be deeply in your debt," Ki said.

"You will be most welcome any time," Chijin said, nodding. "But if I might suggest, I would happily entertain you at my humble home. It is in the Gardens, and there I could see that you meet some of the men who work at the mine."

"I'd be very grateful for an invitation," Ki said. "Any evening that you name."

"Tomorrow, then. Right now, I must excuse myself, for I have heard my pupil entering the front door. But I will be honored to have you remain as long as you wish, and we can take up our conversation later."

"Even if the news we got at the mine wasn't good, I feel a lot better now," Lucy told Jessie as the buggy lurched over the humps and ruts in the road.

"At least you know the worst," Jessie replied. "But I'm not quite sure things are as dark as our friend Manfield painted them."

"What do you mean?" Lucy frowned. "If the mine closes—"

"It's not closed yet," Jessie pointed out.

"Of course not," Lucy agreed. "And he did hold out some hope that they'll be producing ore again."

"Which makes me suspicious, Lucy," Jessie said. "From the little I know about gold mines, when a lode peters out, that's the end of it. Unless the owners of the mine are sure they have another lode, one that hasn't been worked, they'll usually just close down."

"Are you suggesting that Mr. Manfield was holding something back from us?"

"Something of that sort." Jessie nodded. "And he didn't seem to like the idea of having Ki go into the mine and make an inspection."

"But what could he be trying to hide, Jessie?"

"Oh, a number of things. He might know of another lode that never has been worked. If you were convinced that the stock you own is worthless, and he offered to buy it from you for a few cents on the dollar, wouldn't you sell it to him?"

Lucy frowned for a moment as she thought over Jessie's question. Then she nodded. "I suppose I would."

"And if he made the same offer to all the other stockholders wouldn't they be inclined to sell, too?"

"I guess they would."

"And the mine would belong to Manfield then," Jessie went on. "All he'd have to do would be open it up again and he'd be the sole owner, with no dividends to pay out."

"But how could he get away with such a thing, Jessie? That would be—it would be—" Lucy's words tapered off and she sat silently thoughtful.

"It's been done before," Jessie said. "Not too terribly long ago, a gang tried to work a similar scheme on me. Luckily, Ki and I managed to stop them."

"But wouldn't Mr. Manfield be breaking the law if he did something like that?"

"If he handled a scheme of that kind right, I think he could do it without any danger of being punished. If you took him to court, all he'd need to say is that he bought stock he knew was worthless just to help the stockholders make a few dollars out of a dead investment."

"But anyone could see that he'd have been cheating!"

"Not necessarily, Lucy. You'd have to prove that he knew the stock was worthless, and if he had a really good lawyer to defend him, proving that he knew would be almost impossible."

"How can we find out the truth, then?" Lucy asked.

"Well, Ki may find out something if Manfield doesn't think of a way to keep him out of the mine. And we might find out a few things ourselves by asking a few questions at the Prescott bank."

"Is that what you're going to do next?"

"Of course." Jessie glanced at the sun, dropping low now behind the scrub pines that bordered the road. "I don't think we'll get back to town in time to pay a visit to the bank today, but we can certainly do that tomorrow morning before we go back to the mine with Ki."

★

Chapter 8

"It's a genuine pleasure to meet you, Miss Starbuck," the banker said. "Not only because of my admiration for your late father, but because the entire financial world knows of the way you've taken hold of his estate and managed it so superbly."

Jessie had been sizing up the manager of the Bank of Arizona while he talked. James Cassidy was a man still in his early middle years, and from his name she placed him as being descended from a family of what the Britons called "black Irish," because of the dark hair that set them apart in a nation where blond or red hair predominated. Cassidy was tall and slim, and moved quickly. He was clean-shaven, and only a few gray hairs showed at his temples.

"Thank you, Mr. Cassidy," she replied. "I hope I'm not intruding on a busy morning."

"You're not intruding at all," he replied. "Please, sit

down and tell me what we can do to help you."

"I've come to Prescott to try to help a friend," Jessie said as she settled into the chair that Cassidy drew up to his desk. "And I'm hoping that you'll be able to give me some information that I need."

"If I'm correct in assuming that it's information about one of our depositors, I can't really assure you that I'll be able to help," the banker said thoughtfully. "I'm sure that with your experience you're familiar with the rules of confidentiality that we must observe in banking."

"Of course." Jessie nodded. "But I'm not going to ask you to reveal account balances or loans of any of your depositors, Mr. Cassidy."

"That's the sort of information I couldn't give you, but I'd imagine you're aware of that."

"Certainly. And I might also assure you that whatever you tell me will be in strict confidence, just as I'm sure you'll keep my visit confidential."

"Naturally," Cassidy agreed. "Now what is it that you're interested in finding out, Miss Starbuck?"

"What I'd like is as much general information as you can provide about the Empire Mining Company and its president, Mr. Manfield. He must keep the company's funds on deposit here, as this is the only bank in town."

"He does." Cassidy nodded. "But let me ask whether you've discussed this with Manfield."

Jessie shook her head. "No. But my friend and I went out to the mine yesterday, looking for information, and what we got was only the most general sort. I'm not really satisfied with what we were told. I'd hoped to get back to town in time to stop in here, but the bank had already closed."

"You say 'general information,'" Cassidy replied. "That covers a very wide field. Perhaps it would be better if you simply ask me questions. Within the limits of our rules, I'll be glad to answer them."

"There are just a few facts that I think my friend needs to know about the mine," Jessie said. "I haven't any reason to distrust Mr. Manfield, but I'd rather get the answers from a disinterested third party."

"Is this friend you're acting for one of the stockholders?"

"Of course. Unfortunately, Mrs. Chalmers is inexperienced in financial matters. She showed me the last balance sheet the mine enclosed with one of her last dividend payments, but it's very badly out of date."

Cassidy nodded. "I was prepared to hear you say that. In the bank we run into similar situations rather frequently."

When he paused, Jessie went on. "If it would make any difference in your reply, she's here in Prescott now. I came to the Territory with her because she isn't as familiar with mining and finance as I happen to be."

"Very few ladies are, I'd imagine." Cassidy smiled. "Unless your friend happens to be another Hetty Green."

Now it was Jessie who smiled. "There's only one Hetty Green," she said. "And Lucy was a schoolteacher until she married. Her husband died a short time ago, leaving her a quite substantial block of Empire Mining Company stock. I don't think I need to carry her story any further."

"No. Of course, she isn't the only one who was surprised when the Empire suspended dividends." Cassidy was silent for a moment. Then he said slowly, "Suppose you ask the questions, Miss Starbuck, and I'll answer them as fully as I can."

"Is the Empire deeply in debt?" Jessie asked. Then she added, "I imagine that Mr. Manfield has come to your bank for loans."

"Yes. We were happy to oblige him twice, but we were forced to deny his third request," Cassidy replied. "I assume you visited the mine before coming here?"

"Lucy and I went out there yesterday. Mr. Manfield was very obliging, but didn't divulge any details of the Empire's current financial condition."

"Understandably." Cassidy nodded. "But he certainly ought to have furnished a profit-and-loss statement and a balance sheet to Mrs. Chalmers, since she's a shareholder."

"He's promised to let me examine the books," Jessie said. "But I'd like to have some idea of what I should expect to see before Lucy and I go out there again."

"You're familiar with the mine, then."

Jessie shook her head. "Not really. I intend to have someone I can trust to make an examination of the underground works later today. Mr. Manfield told us about the new shaft that's being put down to try to relocate the vein which has been the mine's main producer. I did notice that the company doesn't seem to have a smelter, but I suppose it's located somewhere closer to the railroad line."

"You're very observant, Miss Starbuck. The Empire doesn't own a smelter; it carts its ore to the Iron King Mine, which is about fifteen miles southeast of here."

"That isn't a very efficient operation." Jessie frowned. "I have some firsthand experience in copper mining, and without its smelter my mine in Montana would be nowhere near as profitable. I'm sure the same thing's true about gold mining."

"Certainly. High operating cost is one of the reasons we've felt that any further extension of credit by the bank would be unwise," Cassidy replied. "A smelter would have been a major asset, and if the Empire had one, we'd probably have extended its credit further. But with its only proven gold vein gone, and all its buildings so far from town, all that Manfield has is a hole in the ground. I'm sure you realize that no bank can go very far in loaning money to a business in that situation."

"Yes." Jessie nodded. "And I think you've told me all that I need to know, Mr. Cassidy." She stood up, and the banker also got to his feet. She went on, "I appreciate your help very much. Knowing what you've told me, I can frame the questions I intend to ask Mr. Manfield so that they'll give me any other information I might need."

"There's one other thing you might be interested in knowing before you leave, Miss Starbuck," the banker said. "Most of the gold mines in the Territory have played out; they were working what turned out to be merely shallow alluvial deposits."

"I gather that you don't have a great deal of confidence in gold mining as a sound investment, then?"

"That is something I wouldn't say in public, Miss Starbuck, but besides the Empire and the Iron King, there are only a half-dozen gold mines in Arizona Territory that are still producing. If I was in your friend's position, I'd examine the Empire very thoroughly."

"Oh, I intend to do that." Jessie nodded. "But I appreciate hearing your opinion."

Cassidy went on, "And it might be profitable for you to look at our territorial laws on mining. I think you'd find one pending piece of legislation very interesting."

Jessie got the impression from Cassidy's tone that his words of caution were telling only half the story. She decided that it would be fruitless for her to press for more details, but tucked the advice away in her memory to act on later.

"Thank you again, Mr. Cassidy," she said. "I'll remember what you've told me."

"And if I can be of further help, or if you should need

any other services the bank can provide, I hope you'll call on me."

"Naturally, I will. And if you should get any current information—"

"I'll call on you, in that case," Cassidy promised.

"Do, please. We're at the Burke Hotel. I don't know how long we'll be here, but I want to be absolutely sure of the mine's situation before we leave," Jessie replied. "Good day, Mr. Cassidy."

Back at the hotel, Jessie tapped lightly at the door of Lucy's room. Steven opened the door. "Jessie!" he exclaimed. "Come in. Mother's just been telling me some very good news, and I'm sure she'd want you to hear it, too."

"At least I hope it's good news," Lucy added as Jessie stepped into the room. "While you were away, a lawyer came to the hotel to see me."

"A lawyer? Someone you've known before who found out you were in Prescott?"

"No. I've never seen the man, Jessie. But he must've known something about me, because he offered to exchange my stock in the Empire Mining Company for stock in a brand-new mine that's just opened near Wickenberg."

"That's one of the little towns we passed through on the train while we were on the way here," Steve volunteered. "So it looks like there's still some gold left in the vicinity."

"Perhaps so, Steve," Jessie said. She spoke absently, for alarm bells had begun ringing in her head.

In almost every mailbag which reached her at the Circle Star, there were letters from promoters interested in floating new stock issues for one or another of the Starbuck companies, or touting stocks in firms which had yet to be established. There were times when she was sure that she'd

91

been chosen as a prospect by every pie-in-the-sky stock peddler in the country. Thanks to the caution Alex had taught her, and Ki's memory of her father's experiences with the peddlers of false or useless securities, she'd steered clear of the would-be swindlers.

"What that lawyer told you should give you a pretty good idea who sent him," she told Lucy. "Besides ourselves and the man I've just been talking with at the Bank of Arizona, there's only one person in Prescott who knows about your Empire Mine stock."

"You mean Mr. Manfield?"

Jessie nodded. "Of course."

"But he didn't mention Mr. Manfield's name." Lucy frowned.

"I'm sure he'd've been careful not to," Jessie said. "Go on, Lucy. What did this lawyer tell you?"

"Well, the new mine he mentioned is just getting started, but Mr. Rourke says it's going to be very profitable."

"And did he happen to mention knowing that your Empire stock isn't paying any dividends now?"

"Why, yes, he did. How did you know?" Lucy frowned.

Leaving Lucy's question unanswered, Jessie went on, "Did he say why he was offering to exchange your Empire stock when he knows it's not bringing you any income?"

"Yes. He told me the new mine needs hoists and ore-carts and some other machinery and equipment, and the cheapest way to get it was to trade stock in the new mine for all the Empire stock. Then the equipment will belong to the new company."

"He didn't suggest that you check out his story with a bank, or give you any references?"

"No. But he's a lawyer, Jessie! Lawyers don't go around swindling people!"

"Some do, I'm afraid." Jessie smiled wryly. "There are bad apples in every barrel. But let's see just what this Mr. Rourke's offer actually amounted to. He didn't offer to buy your stock outright, for cash, did he?"

"No. He made sure I understood that I'd get stock in the new mine in return for my Empire stock."

"I hope you didn't agree to do it."

"Of course I didn't, Jessie!" Lucy protested. "Why, you know I wouldn't do that without talking to you about it."

"Did you tell this lawyer to come back, then?"

"No, not exactly. When I said I'd have to talk to you, he told me he'd come back later today, just before supper, to get my answer. Now I'll know what to say when he shows up."

Steven broke into the conversation between Jessie and Lucy to say, "It sounds to me like you're suspicious of this fellow Rourke, Jessie. Of course, I wasn't here when he talked to Mother, but his offer sounded all right to me when she told me about it."

"Perhaps I'm just being over-suspicious," Jessie said. "But before you talk to this lawyer again— By the way, what's his first name?"

"Rourke," Lucy told her. "Donald Rourke."

Jessie went on, "Before you talk to this Mr. Rourke again, we'd better find out a little bit about him. We can ask—"

She broke off when a knock sounded at the door. Steven went to open it. Ki came in.

"A conference?" He smiled and added, "I tapped at the door of your room, Jessie, and then tried Steven's. Has something new come up while I was away?"

"Nothing that can't wait," Jessie told him. "What did you find out at the capitol?"

"Much more than I'd expected when you asked me to

get a list of the mine's stockholders from the Securities Commission file," Ki replied.

"Let me guess at something," Jessie said. "There've been a lot of transfers of Empire stock lately."

Ki nodded. "That's a good guess, Jessie. "Yes, quite a few. Some of them for cash, some in exchange for stock in other mines."

"And almost all of the exchanges have been made by Edgar Manfield?" she went on.

"If I didn't know better, I'd think you've seen that file of stock transfers yourself." Ki frowned. "Most of them were made to Manfield by people in the East and Midwest. He seems to have set out to get full control of the Empire Mining Company."

Jessie looked at Lucy and said, "That might explain why the lawyer called on you. I'd say that Ki's right, and there must be a reason for what he's doing."

"I think I've found the reason, Jessie," Ki said quietly.

"This gets more interesting as we go along," Jessie commented. "Suppose you tell us what else you've come up with."

"I took the hint you got from the banker, and paid a visit to the Attorney General's office while I was in the capitol," Ki went on. "When I asked the clerk about new laws affecting mining that are scheduled to be voted on, he got out a file of about twenty. It seems that there've been so many gold-mining swindlers and so many attempted swindles lately that the legislature's trying to stop them."

"Aren't there already laws against fraudulent stock schemes here in Arizona Territory?" Jessie frowned.

"Of course." Ki nodded. "But the clerk I talked with said that convictions for fraud are very hard to get. But to get right to the point, one of those proposed new laws would keep any principal stockholder or officer of a bankrupt gold mine from owning or controlling another mine in the territory for twenty years."

Jessie thought for a moment, then said slowly, "So if that law is passed, if Manfield should close the Empire and declare it bankrupt, it would be impossible for him to get control of another mine right away."

"That would be the case, all right." Ki nodded. "And he'd have to own enough stock to outvote the other stockholders, like Mrs. Chalmers, if they tried to put the mine into bankruptcy."

"But if I'd sold my stock, I wouldn't care what he did," Lucy pointed out.

"You're overlooking something," Steven said quickly. "What if they find that gold vein they're looking for, or stumble onto another one as good? If you'd sold your stock, you'd be out in the cold."

"We're going to have to look into all these things that've come up since we got here," Jessie said decisively. "And the place to start looking is that mine."

"I've been thinking the same thing," Ki said. "And it seems to me that the only way we can learn about the mine is to get into it."

"But from what Mother and Jessie told us, Manfield isn't going to let that happen," Steven put in.

"Manfield doesn't know me," Ki replied quickly. Then he turned to Jessie and said, "I'm sure that I can arrange to get a firsthand look, Jessie."

"How?"

"Remember, I told you that Chijin Yamata has asked me to his home in Chinese Gardens this evening, so I can talk to some of the Orientals who work at the mine," Ki reminded her. "I was intending only to ask them some questions, but I'm sure that at least one of them will know how I can find a way to get into it."

"Secretly?" Jessie frowned.

"Of course. Perhaps at night, when the men aren't at work. I'm sure that under the conditions out there Manfield isn't working two or three shifts of men underground."

"Suppose he is?"

"Why, I'll pay one of the miners to let me take his place for a shift or two," Ki told her. "As far as I can see, the best way to find out what we want to know is for one of us to get inside that mine, Jessie."

"Yes, I suppose that's true," Jessie agreed after a moment of thoughtful silence. "But I still don't like it, Ki. If you go into that mine posing as one of the miners, I intend to be somewhere close by, in case there's trouble."

"If you think you might run into trouble, Ki, I'll be glad to go with you when you go into the mine," Steven volunteered.

"I appreciate your offer, Steven," Ki said quickly. "And I'm sure Jessie does, too. But it's not practical. If only Orientals are working at the mine, you'd stand out like a raisin in a bowl of rice."

"I suppose I would, at that," Steven agreed. "But I feel useless, there's so little I can do to help."

"Don't worry," Jessie said quickly. "There'll be plenty for all of us to do, if my suspicions are correct. But it's too early for us to make any plans. We'd better wait until we find out what develops from Ki's visit to his new friend this evening. Then we can work out what our next move should be."

"We were going out with Ki to the mine this afternoon," Lucy reminded Jessie. "Aren't we going, then?"

"I think we'd better change our plans," Jessie said thoughtfully. "Suppose you and I go alone, Lucy. With what we know now about Manfield's maneuvers and what we've begun to suspect, we're a lot better equipped to question him."

"I agree with Jessie," Ki put in. "For all we know right this minute, there may not be anything wrong with the shaft that Manfield told you they had to abandon."

"Yes, swindlers' minds don't work like ours," Jessie said. "And I feel just like you do, Ki; the risk's worth taking. Go ahead with your plan. But when and if you do go into that mine, I'm going to be waiting in some hiding-place close by."

"You won't be waiting alone, Jessie," Steven volunteered. "I'll be waiting with you."

Chapter 9

"There was no need for you to go to the expense of renting a horse," Chijin told Ki. "I would have been glad to take you back to town later."

"My expense was nothing, and you lose no face by letting me return alone," Ki assured his host. "I can stay in bed late tomorrow morning; you must start early because you have your businesses to look after."

Ki was sitting beside the restaurant operator on the seat of the buggy, taking stock as best he could in the gathering darkness of the houses that made up the Chinese Gardens. He could see very few details of the little dwellings, for they were scattered willy-nilly in the scanty low-growing brush, and the road was a winding one, little more than a trail.

Most of the small, neat, two- and three-room dwellings stood some distance away from the road. Lights were already showing in many of the houses, and to the east beyond the dwellings a ragged line of high hills, not quite imposing enough to be called mountains, was merging with the darkening sky.

Chijin pulled up the buggy in front of one of the houses that stood only a short distance from the lane, and the horse on a leader behind the vehicle stamped on the packed soil of the road. Peering through the gloom that was settling in, Ki saw that Chijin's house was a bit larger than any of the others visible. Even in the failing light he could see that it was neatly painted and well cared-for.

"If I'd been thoughtful," Ki said, "I would have refused your invitation, but it didn't occur to me that evening is your busy time."

"I have good help to look after the tea-house," Chijin said as they walked toward the door of the bungalow. "I often leave them in the evening to come home early. I'd have preferred to live in town, but as the master has said, 'there is no peace in a house that is not surrounded by those of friends.'"

Before Ki and his host reached the door, it swung open and two women came onto the narrow porch. Both of them wore American-style clothing, and both bowed as Ki and Chijin mounted the steps to the porch.

"I present to you my wife, Sai Lin, and my daughter, Yin Chee," Chijin said. Then, turning to the women, he went on, "Our guest Ki, who honors our humble house this evening."

As the women bowed and repeated Ki's name, Chijin gestured for Ki to step inside. He entered a room decorated and furnished in the oriental style. It was almost bare of furniture; Ki saw only three chairs with small tabourets close to them, and a large, low table in its center, with cushions rather than chairs at its sides. There were two framed pictures on the walls, and several lush tapestries. In

99

several of the woven works, gold threads glinted in the soft light shed through tall parchment-shaded lamps that stood in each corner.

Chijin interrupted Ki's inspection. He said, "We eat as a family, even on the few occasions when we have guests. Sai Lin and Yin Chee will serve us; then, in the way of American women, they will join us at the table."

Ki nodded and sat down on the cushion that Chijin indicated, folding his legs in the oriental style. Then for the next hour he recalled memories that he'd thought were long-banished, as Sai Lin and Yin Chee offered them bowls of thick *miso-shuri* soup served over well-coated *udan* noodles, and then filled fresh plates piled with *mizu-tabo* beef shreds stirred into the finely textured noodles called *norimaki*.

After the meal, as they were sipping *lun ching* tea with *semki,* Sai Lin asked Ki, "You have no wife in this place where you live, Texas?"

"No," Ki replied. "But there will be a time when I must look for one."

"Is it as lonely in Texas as it is here?" Yin Chee asked.

"Much more." Ki nodded. "Places there are even farther apart than here. But work keeps me busy."

"Are there no towns close to the ranch where you live?" She frowned.

Ki shook his head. "No. To go to a town, we must ride for a half-day on a train."

"Why, that is even lonelier than I had thought!" she exclaimed. "What do you do for company?"

"There is enough work to be done to keep me busy. Guests visit the ranch. And when Miss Starbuck travels on business, I go with her, as I've come here to Prescott."

Sai Lin broke in on their conversation. "Come, Yin

Chee," she said. "Your father and Ki have business to look after, and we have work to do ourselves."

"I have been enjoying your visit and our talk," Chijin said as the women vanished into the rear of the house. "And while we talked, more time has passed than I realized. It is time for us to go, if you wish to ask questions of the men who work at the mine."

"But I haven't thanked your wife and daughter for this delicious dinner," Ki told him. "It would be discourteous for me to fail to do that before we leave."

"They will understand why we have gone, and you can tell them when we come back. They heard the wagon which brings the men from the mine pass by, just as I did. The miners will go to bed very soon; they must start for the mine before daybreak."

"And that, I understand." Ki nodded. "That's when our days start at the ranch. Let's go, then."

Outside, only the faint sliver of the moon in its last phase lighted the zigzag path on which Chijin led Ki. Many of the houses they passed were already dark, and most of those in which lights showed had shutters over their windows. Ki caught the scent of a corral. A few moments later he heard the whuffling of horses and a few words of low-voiced conversation. Then he could see the silhouettes of four or five men outlined against the clear, starry sky. Chijin spoke then.

"Here is the man I told you wishes to ask questions about the mine," he said. "Go ahead, Ki. This is Tao Feng, this is Sung Di, there is Chan Sing, and the other is Kin Chi. All of them understand why you have asked that they say nothing to the other miners about meeting them."

"Have any of you heard the name of Starbuck?" Ki asked.

Chan Sing said promptly, "Of course. He is the man

101

who paid the passage of my father and mother when they came here to America."

Tao Feng responded almost as quickly. "When I was a child in San Francisco, he gave my mother the money to buy a proper funeral for my father."

"I did not know him, but I have heard his name," Sung Di volunteered.

"And I have heard good things said of him by our people," Kin Chi said.

Ki concealed his surprise at the answers that Chan Sing and Tao Feng had given to his question. He'd known many instances when Alex had helped both Japanese and Chinese to migrate to the United States, but the names of these men were strange to him.

"Then you will understand when I tell you that it was Alex Starbuck who brought me to America," Ki went on. "I served him until he was killed by his enemies. Now I serve his daughter. She came here with a friend who has money invested in the mine where you work. I'm sure you know of the trouble there."

There was a moment of silence. Then Sung Di replied, "All of us know that the big shaft is closed, and that we are digging another."

"I am still working in the old tunnel," Kin Chi volunteered. "We are digging along the face of the big stone that has closed it."

"That is what I am doing, too," Chan Sing said.

"I am in the same gang with Sung Di," Tao Feng told Ki. "The foreman who was our boss wanted me to go with him when he left to be boss of the new shaft. He said that I would make a bigger wage, but when he told me that if I went to the new job I could no longer come home to my family when the day was finished, I stayed with my old gang."

102

"Why could you not have come home?" Ki asked. "Your friends here are working on the new shaft."

"That is not the shaft my foreman talked about," Tao Feng replied, "it is the new one they have started, away from the one that they began to dig after the old main shaft was blocked by the stone."

"Then there are two new main shafts?" Ki asked, keeping the puzzlement that had swept over him out of his voice.

"Of course," Tao Feng said. "Before my foreman warned me to say nothing, I had already told my friends here. The next day, after he had ordered me to say nothing, we agreed we would not talk of it, even among ourselves."

"You were ordered not to mention it?" Ki went on, keeping his voice from reflecting his surprise. "Then why have you told me?"

"Because Chijin told us that you and Miss Starbuck need to know. We do not forget what her father did for us," Kin Chi put in quickly.

"Since you've gone this far, I don't suppose you'll mind telling me why they're digging the shaft your foreman asked you to work in?" Ki asked, his voice as unruffled as ever.

"That, I do not know. No one knows," Tao Feng replied.

"This is a true thing," Kin Chi agreed. "None of us except Tao has even heard about it."

"And except to you, Ki, we have said nothing about it," Sung Di seconded.

His voice revealing his disgruntlement, Tao Feng added, "Even here in America, we are still treated as coolies."

"Not by everyone," Ki replied. "I have met some who do not look on us as inferiors."

"Perhaps. But there are not many," Chan Sing said. Then he went on, "We have told you all that we know of the mine, Ki. It is late, and we do not have much time left to sleep."

Ki nodded. "Of course." He reached into his pocket, but Tao Feng took hold of his wrist.

"We want nothing from you or from Jessica Starbuck, Ki," the miner said. "We have tried to help you because of what Alex Starbuck did for us."

"Then I can only thank you for the help you have given me," Ki told the man. "I will not forget, and neither will Jessie Starbuck. Now, we will go and leave you to your rest."

After the miners had gone, Ki and Chijin started back toward the house. In most of the other dwellings the lights had been extinguished now.

"I will go in only long enough to thank Sai Lin and Yin Chee for dinner," Ki said as they walked. "It's getting late, and Jessie will be wondering what's happened to me."

"You are welcome to stay as long as you wish, Ki," Chijin told him. "We have had no time yet to talk about the changes that are taking place in *Goju* here in America, where there are so many guns."

"Yes, we must talk of that later," Ki said. "It is something I have noticed, too. I have put aside my *bo* and *nun-chaka,* and more than ever I depend on my *shuriken.*"

They'd reached Chijin's house by now. Though all the little dwellings close by were now dark, lights still glowed in its windows. When they went in, Sai Lin rose from one of the chairs and bowed to greet them.

"You will want tea," she said. "I will bring it."

"Please don't trouble yourself with tea," Ki told her. "It will be very late when I get back to the hotel, and my friends must be wondering right now what has happened to me. I only came in to thank you and Yin Chee for the excellent dinner."

"Yin Chee has already gone to bed," Sai Lin said. "But I will tell her." She bowed again and went on, "I am honored that you have enjoyed our modest food."

"And I that you have honored our poor house with your visit," Chijin added, bowing to complete the traditional ritual offered a departing guest.

"It is I who has been honored," Ki said as returned their bows. "We will meet again later, I am sure." Then, businesslike again, he added, "Please don't bother to come with me to my horse. I will visit you soon at your *do,* and we will talk more then."

Outside, the cool night breeze had begun to stir the air. Ki walked the short distance to his horse, and was pulling its reins away from the hitchrail when the low-growing brush beyond the rail rustled. Dropping the reins, Ki slid a *shuriken* from his vest pocket as he peered into the darkness. Then a woman's light voice, pitched in a whisper, reached his ears.

"Don't be alarmed, Ki. It is me, Yin Chee."

"Yin Chee? I thought you'd gone to bed."

"So did Sai Lin," Yin Chee went on as she emerged from the brush, the light-colored kimono she wore outlining her against the dark, stunted clumps. "I knew that if I waited in the house with her for you and Father to get back, I wouldn't have a chance to see you alone before you left."

"Why should you wish to see me alone?"

"You shouldn't have to ask me that, Ki. Or did my posing at supper fool you?"

"I didn't notice you posing," Ki replied. He'd recovered quickly from his first surprise. Already a suspicion of what was in Yin Chee's mind was growing in his own.

"I didn't expect you to," Yin Chee told him. "Mother and Father keep hoping to find another husband for me. They don't tell anyone that I'm a widow, and they still treat me like a little girl when we have guests."

"They didn't give me even a hint that you'd been married," Ki said. "But from what you've said, I don't suppose that would've been unusual."

"No." Yin Chee hesitated for a moment. Then, with more than a touch of defiance in her voice, she went on, "So when I can get away from them for a while, I look for a man to ease the itching between my legs. Would you like to do that, Ki?"

"Right here and now?" he asked.

"Of course. Where else is there?"

Ki was now past his initial surprise, and Yin Chee's very frankness had begun reminding him that he'd been celibate for too long a time. He asked, "You don't mind the ground?"

"Of course I do. But there are other ways."

Yin Chee came close to Ki and began caressing his crotch. He made no effort to stop her. Her frank invitation and the vision it had brought into his mind were having an effect. He made no effort to stop her when she began caressing his crotch. Then caution spoke.

"We're very exposed here," he said. "Suppose Chijin or Sai Ling looked out a window?"

"They sleep in a room on the other side of the house."

"But isn't there some kind of shelter close by?" he asked.

"Just the bushes, but they'll hide us well enough." While she was speaking, Yin Chee stopped caressing Ki's growing erection and took his arm. She led him toward a thick clump of young trees sprouting a short distance from the road. As they walked, she went on, "We can't do the

106

splitting of the bamboo on this rough ground, but I don't care for that too much. I'll play the mare and you be the stallion."

They reached the little thicket, and Yin Chee released Ki's arm and let the kimono slide off her shoulders. There was no moon, but the starlit night was bright. Ki could see the ruddy tips of Yin Chee's small breasts, pebbled in the gloom, and the dark triangle of her pubic brush.

She stepped closer to him and fumblingly tugged at his sash until she'd released it, then helped him shrug out of his loose jacket and pulled the knot of his waistband until his baggy trousers slid to the ground. When Yin Chee began fumbling at the overlapped band of the narrow sash that Ki wore as a cache-sexe his erection was already pushing at the narrow strip of cloth. When he felt her futile efforts, Ki brushed her hands aside and pushed the cache-sexe down over his hips.

"Aiee!" Yin Chee gasped when she saw his erection spring up. "You are a stallion indeed, Ki! Hurry! I want to be the mare and feel you mounting me!"

Turning her back to him, Yin Chee bent forward until her head almost touched the ground. Ki was in no mood to hesitate now. He went in with a single thrust and Yin Chee did indeed snort like a mare as she felt his deep, strong penetration. She writhed for a moment; then, as Ki began stroking, he felt her grow tense. He was plunging now, like the stallion she'd urged him to be, and Yin Chee was rearing back to meet his rhythmic strokes.

"Faster!" she urged in a breathy whisper. "Never before now have I been the mare to such a stud!"

Spurred by her urgency, Ki did as she asked. He heard the cry of completion forming in her throat long before he was ready to match her climax, and he hesitated for a moment, buried deep within her. Then Yin Chee twisted fran-

tically in Ki's arms and began quivering. Her cries broke
the stillness, and her body convulsed and shook. Ki
grasped her hips and held her closer to him, burying himself in her while she writhed and gasped and shuddered to
her climax.

When her ecstatic cries had died away, Yin Chee moved
as though to break away from him, but Ki tightened his
grip and lifted her bodily, then turned her in midair to face
him, his shaft still impaling her. Yin Chee realized what he
intended, and locked her legs around him. Then, as Ki
cradled her buttocks in his strong hands and started stroking again, she tightened her legs to pull him into her more
deeply as he thrust.

"Aiee!" she breathed. "Now I am both mare and
woman, and you are both man and stallion!"

Ki maintained his pace until he too was rising to the
peak that Yin Chee had just passed. He felt her beginning
to quiver in his hands, and in the moments before his own
completion he did as Yin Chee had asked. When he felt her
climactic quivering beginning to seize her again, he drove
to his own completion, and Yin Chee's ecstasy peaked with
his.

As they reached the endless moment that is so brief, he
pulled her to him and clasped her close while they sighed
almost in unison. Then Ki slid his arms up Yin Chee's
ribcage to her armpits and held her until she lowered her
legs and stepped away from him.

"If you can stay longer—" she began, but Ki broke in.

"No, Yin Chee. Much as I'd like to, it's not possible. I
must tell the others what I learned tonight from the miners,
and we will need to make plans."

"I will not see you tomorrow, then?"

"No. The next day, perhaps, or the day after." Ki was
gathering up his clothing as he spoke.

When Yin Chee saw him begin to dress, she realized that their moment had indeed ended. She picked up her kimono and shrugged into it. She said, "Good night, then, Ki. I will think about the time when you return while I am waiting for you."

By the time Yin Chee had disappeared into the darkness, Ki had finished dressing and was starting for his horse. The road back to Prescott seemed much longer than it had when he'd come to the Chinese Gardens, but he finally reached the livery stable, left his horse, and walked the short distance to the hotel. The transom above Jessie's door was dark; so were those over the doors of the rooms occupied by Steve and Lucy.

When he went into his own room and lighted the lamp, the first thing he saw was a note from Jessie. It was very short, only one word: "Tomorrow."

Suppressing a sigh of relief that there would be no long discussion to end the night, Ki quickly stepped out of his clothes and went to bed.

★

Chapter 10

"I can't believe that such a thing would be possible, Ki!" Jessie exclaimed after Ki finished talking. He, Jessie, Lucy, and Steve were sitting at the breakfast table in a secluded corner of the hotel's dining room, and Ki had just finished outlining what he'd learned the night before from the men who worked at the Empire. "How could Manfield expect to have a crew of men out there, digging the main shaft for a new mine, without anybody in Prescott finding out about it?"

"I'd say he's managed to keep it a secret pretty well, so far," Ki replied. "When you come down to it, Jessie, the mine is so far off the beaten track that it's quite possible."

Jessie shook her head. "No, Ki. If those men you talked to last night told you, they must've told others."

"Perhaps so," Ki agreed. "But you know just as well as I do how close-mouthed we Orientals can be. They might've told one or two of their neighbors, but as far as

110

the people here in Prescott are concerned, the Chinese Gardens might as well be on the moon."

"Suppose what you've said is true," Jessie went on thoughtfully. "Even if that second—no, it'd be the third—mine shaft is a secret now, I doubt that it will be much longer."

"I won't argue that with you," Ki agreed. "Sooner or later, someone's going to start talking."

Steve broke in. "Jessie, that might explain why the lawyer came here yesterday trying to buy mother's stock."

"Yes, I'm sure there's a connection," Jessie agreed. "And we're bound to find out what it is, sooner or later."

"Better sooner than later," Ki told her. "But while I was riding back to town last night, I thought of a way to find out a great deal more."

"How?" Jessie asked.

"I'll simply arrange with one of the miners I met last night to take his place for a few days. Once I've learned the way the land lays, I'll find a way to get to somebody in the crew that's putting down the new shaft, and find out exactly what's going on."

Jessie shook her head. "You'd never get by with something as obvious as that, Ki. You'd be spotted in a minute."

"No, I don't think I would," Ki replied. "I don't know how many men are working on the new shaft, but there'd have to be twenty or thirty. I might not be able to fool their foreman very long, but it's only going to take a little while to find out what we need to know."

"Ki, it's simply too dangerous!" Jessie objected. "I don't like the idea at all!"

Lucy had been listening to Jessie and Ki without speaking. Now she said, "It does sound terribly risky, Ki. And since the only reason you'd have for doing it would be to help me with my problem, I'd feel responsible if you ran into trouble."

"Of course it's dangerous!" Steve put in. "But I'm on Ki's side. If I knew as much as he does about mining, I'd go into that mine shaft myself."

While her companions talked, Jessie had been thinking. She said, "I'll agree with you about one thing, Ki. Your idea's a good one, and I don't suppose there'd be too much trouble in carrying it out. But I'd like it a lot better if there was someone watching outside that new mine shaft who'd be on hand to jump in and give you a hand if trouble started."

"Do you really think that's necessary, Jessie?" Ki asked. "We've always been able to handle our problems by ourselves, without depending on others."

"Perhaps not always, but most of the time." Jessie smiled. "This situation's a bit different, though. I still want someone we know we can trust to back you up this time."

"Why can't I do that?" Steve asked.

"No, Steve!" Lucy protested. "You haven't had the experience Ki and Jessie have in this rough Western country."

Ki nodded. "I'm afraid Lucy's right."

Jessie broke in. "Of course she is, and so is Ki. It's not any reflection on your courage, Steve. I agree with Ki. His idea to go into the mine is the best way to find out what's really going on. But Lucy's right, too. We need somebody who not only knows the country, but who can handle a gun in case trouble does develop."

"Who's that going to be?" Steve asked.

"I don't know," Jessie replied. "But I do know who can tell us where to find somebody who'll be able to do the job—Mr. Cassidy, at the bank. In his job, he'd know almost anything there is to know about Prescott. I'd trust him to recommend the kind of man we need."

112

"Let's go talk to him, then," Lucy suggested.

"We will, of course," Jessie told her friend. "But that's the second item on our list, Lucy. We've got to go back out to the mine this morning and talk to Manfield again."

"Didn't we find out everything we needed to know yesterday?" Lucy frowned.

"Almost everything," Jessie replied. "But we'd better make absolutely sure that he's really trying to work the kind of swindle we suspect. If what we suspect is true, we can force him to move. Then we'll be able to get the evidence we need to put this whole affair into the hands of the local court."

"I like your idea, Jessie," Lucy said. "I don't mind telling you that this is worrying me a great deal."

"Then let's get started," Jessie suggested.

"Suppose Steve and I go along with you," Ki offered. "We can scout around while you and Lucy are with Manfield, and see if we can uncover some solid evidence to back our suspicions."

"Of course," Jessie agreed. "You should know the country around the mine anyhow, if we're going to carry out your plan." She stood up and went on briskly, "There's no use in delaying. The sooner we start, the faster we're going to get everything straightened out."

When they reached the fork in the road where the Empire Mining Company's sign marked their turn-off, Jessie pulled up and waited for Ki and Steve to bring their livery horses alongside the buggy.

"I hope your friends gave you some idea where to look for the new mine shaft," Jessie said to Ki.

She looked at the country ahead of them, the sign, and the road to the mine where it curved and disappeared into the dense growth of scrub pines and junipers. The litter that

113

had been discarded beside the narrow, deeply-rutted traces through the years were the only signs visible to indicate that civilization had swept across the area.

"I suppose you know where to start looking," she added.

"Not exactly," Ki told her. "But from what the men I was talking to last night said, it'll be somewhere north of the present mine. All that Steve and I can do is circle around the mine and then zigzag through the hills to the north until we run across the fresh diggings."

"When Lucy and I finish our talk with Manfield, we'll go back to town, then," Jessie said. "We'll be at the hotel when you get through scouting."

"It's not likely that we'll get back until dark," Ki told her. "Unless we're very lucky."

Ki wheeled his horse and rejoined Steve. Jessie watched the pair as they talked for a moment; then, when Ki and Steve had toed their horses ahead and disappeared into the trees, she slapped the reins over the horse's back and guided the animal onto the road to the mine.

This time the distance did not seem as great as it had on their first visit. When they glimpsed the mine's office building through the trees ahead, Jessie turned to Lucy.

"When Manfield learns that we've found out about his scheme, he'll probably try to persuade you to sell your stock to him," she warned her friend. "But no matter what he says, don't make the mistake of accepting any offer he makes. I'm convinced that Manfield is behind the lawyer who wanted to buy you out."

"Don't worry," Lucy said, nodding. "You ought to remember from your school days that I can be very stubborn when I want to be."

"Yes." Jessie smiled. "I remember quite well how you ruled the classes I was in. Until I got to know you better, and came to admire you, I thought you were a very mean person, Lucy."

"And I'm going to be just as firm with Mr. Manfield as I was with you," Lucy promised. "Just wait and see."

They reached the mine office and went inside. The elderly clerk was still working on his ledger, and the door to Manfield's offices was closed. The clerk stood up and came to the counter that divided the room when he saw Lucy and Jessie.

"I suppose you've come to see Mr. Manfield again," he said.

"If he's not busy," Lucy replied.

"There's a gentleman with him now, but they should finish their business soon. If you don't mind waiting a few minutes—" He broke off as the door of Manfield's office opened. The mine manager came out, accompanied by a stout, well dressed man. Both men were smiling broadly when they opened the door, but the grins vanished from their faces when they saw Lucy and Jessie.

Lucy's eyes widened and she whispered to Jessie, "That's Mr. Rourke, the man who wanted to buy my stock yesterday. You were right, Jessie! Mr. Manfield's trying to swindle me!"

Before Lucy would say anything more, or Jessie could reply, Manfield turned to Rourke.

"No, sir!" he said loudly. "I'll repeat what I told you a minute ago—my stock in the Empire mine is not for sale! I intend to make this mine profitable again. That's the least I can do for the fine people who own stock in it! Good day, sir!"

Rourke's jaw had dropped for an instant when Manfield first started talking; then he'd gotten his clue. When the mine manager fell silent, he said, "I'm sorry you feel that way, Mr. Manfield, but I can tell by the tone of your voice that you mean what you say. That being the case, I won't press my offer, and won't disturb you again."

As Rourke hurried out the door, Manfield turned to Jessie and Lucy. "Can you imagine! That man had the nerve to suggest that I sell him the little bit of stock I own in the Empire Mine! But I suppose you heard what I told him."

"Yes, indeed," Jessie replied. "We heard it very clearly, just as you intended us to."

"I'm not sure I understand what you mean, Miss Starbuck," Manfield frowned.

"I think you do," Jessie said levelly. "But perhaps we'd better go into our office to continue our discussion." She took Lucy's arm and tugged her along as they swept past Manfield into his office. They stood waiting while Manfield closed the door and moved to his desk. Jessie went on, "I'm not in the habit of beating around bushes, Mr. Manfield. There are some very odd things happening here."

"I'm not sure that I understand you, Miss Starbuck," he replied. "Perhaps you'd better explain."

Jessie's voice was icy as she said, "I don't think you need any explanation from Mrs. Chalmers or me. You gave us a very good example of quick thinking a moment ago, but that's beside the point."

"I'm still at a loss, Miss Starbuck," Manfield said. "The man who just left came to me with an offer to buy my Empire Mining Company stock. You heard me refuse to sell it to him. I don't see that I have anything further to explain."

"Then I'm sure you won't object if one of the attorneys from the Territorial Mining Commission calls on you later today." Jessie said calmly. "Because when we leave here, Mrs. Chalmers is going to the capitol to file a formal request for the Commission to make a thorough investigation

116

of this company's books and all its other records. I'm sure that as a stockholder in the company, she has that right."

"Hold on!" Manfield gasped. "You can't do that! We— that is, the Empire has a perfectly clear record!"

"Then you certainly can't object, can you?" Jessie countered. "If you have nothing to hide, the investigators won't find anything wrong."

"But that—I mean, that will—" Manfield stammered for a moment. Then, with an almost visible effort, he recovered at least part of the poise he'd lost. He went on, "Miss Starbuck, you have no standing in this. You don't own any of our stock, so I don't owe you any explanation. As for Mrs. Chalmers, if she's worried, I'll be very glad to relieve her of her concern about its value." He turned to Lucy and continued. "I will be very glad to buy your stock myself, Mrs. Chalmers. Nothing could be fairer than that, now, could it?"

Lucy looked at Jessie, a question in her eyes. Jessie shook her head and Lucy faced Manfield again. She said, "I don't want to sell my stock, Mr. Manfield. Not to you or to anyone else. I'm not very clever at business affairs, but I haven't lost my senses. I'm sure that if you're willing to buy my stock, you're not just acting out of charity."

"I think that settles any business we might've come here for," Jessie said quickly. "Come, Lucy. Let's go back to town and get an investigation started." As she and Lucy went out the door, she turned to the clerk, who'd resumed his work on the ledger. She said, "I don't believe I've ever learned your name."

"Rogers, ma'am. Edmund Rogers," the man said.

Jessie went on, "Then, Mr. Rogers, I'd advise you not to let Mr. Manfield make any alterations on your books. There'll be an investigator from the Territorial Mining Commission coming in to examine them later. Mr. Manfield may be in trouble, and you'll certainly be joining him if you allow him to change any old entries or make any new ones."

"But he's my boss, ma'am!" the clerk objected.

"He may not be for long," Jessie said. "But it's up to you whether you follow my advice. All I can do is warn you." She turned back to Lucy and went on, "Come on. Let's go."

"I'm really new at this kind of thing, Ki," Steve said as they left Jessie and rode into the brush. "This country we're in is so different from New England that I get a little bit nervous just looking at it."

"I used to feel the same way when I first came to America with Alex Starbuck," Ki replied. "Japan's even smaller than New England, and almost every inch of it was settled even before America was discovered. But you'll get used to it."

"I hope so. But it seems to me like we're sort of looking for a needle in a haystack. Where do we start looking for a new mine shaft?"

"We've already started." Ki smiled. "All I know is that the new mine Manfield's being so secretive about is somewhere north of the present one."

"If that's the only thing we know, how can we ever hope to find it in this underbrush?"

As he spoke, Steven waved his arm to indicate the area they were riding across. Small stands of tall pines rose here and there, and many large stretches of ground were covered by clusters of greasewood, or expanses of thickly clumped junipers that grew higher than their heads. Occasionally a massive boulder or a formation of solid rock broke the dense junipers.

"We'll have to manage to stay in sight of each other,"

Ki said. "But mainly what we'd better do is be sure that we push on to the north. We know that the new shaft that Chijin's friends told me about is in that direction. As soon as we get past the Empire's office, we'll start zigzagging from the southwest to the northeast until we find what we're looking for."

Steven smiled. "You make it sound simple. I hope that's really the way it is. If it wasn't for the sun, I couldn't tell east from west in this tangle."

"That's enough to go by," Ki replied. "We'll ride into the sun for . . . oh, a mile or so, then turn around and ride away from it. If we separate and just stay in sight of each other, we'll cover a lot more ground."

"And you think we can really find the place?"

"We ought not have too much trouble. All that we really have to do is keep looking. There's one thing in our favor —when a mine shaft's being dug, there's no way to hide the piles of dirt that come out of it."

"And when we find the new mine, what do we do then?"

"We'll have to decide that after we've found it. If we're lucky enough to run across it before Jessie and your mother start back to Prescott, we can hurry back and tell Jessie what we've seen, then decide what's best to do."

"Lead on, then, Ki," Steve said. "I'm with you."

"But not for long. We'd better split up, but keep in sight of one another. In this broken-up country, that mine shaft might be down in one of these valleys, and we could ride past it without ever seeing it if we're too far apart."

Even before he'd finished talking, Ki was scanning the area around them. He pointed to the line of a jagged ridge that broke their limited view of the horizon about three-quarters of a mile to the north.

"Suppose I ride along that ridge and you stay on this one

119

we're on now. I'm used to getting around on horseback and you're not, so I'll be able to cover ground a bit faster than you can."

"And what do you want me to do?" Steve asked.

"Just head into the sun and keep on the crest of this ridge. Don't go further than a mile, and as soon as I get to the one over there, you'll be able to see me, and we can wave signals back and forth when it's time to turn back."

Ki watched Steve for a few moments as the younger man rode off, then reined his horse around and started descending the slope to the valley that separated him from the ridge that was his goal. Picking up its hooves gingerly, moving at a slow walk, the horse started down the steep slope.

As the animal braced its legs against the downward slant, Ki saw that the footing was even more treacherous than he'd anticipated. The animal dug its hooves into the thin layer of rock-studded soil, and slid with its belly almost touching the ground when it could not walk. At last Ki reached the bottom. He looked back to locate Steve.

For a moment, he thought he'd lost his companion. Then, he saw Steve emerging from a thick stand of juniper, looking over his shoulder as his eyes searched the valley for Ki. Ki waved and started up the slope to the next ridge.

Though the grade on that side of the valley was even steeper than the one he'd just descended, the going was easier. He reached the spine and looked again for his companion, scanning the country that was now behind him until he could see Steve's head above a strip where low-growing, brushy greasewood predominated. A bit relieved to see that the novice was doing so well, Ki reined his horse up the slope.

His progress uphill was easier, for there was less impeding brush on the canyon's side. He reached the top and reined in the livery horse while he twisted in the saddle to locate Steve again, but heavy clumps of brush hid the crest. Satisfied that when he got to the higher top of the next ridge Steve could see him easily, Ki turned the horse down the valley's sloping side, and without stopping nudged his mount to start up the next slope.

When he saw that the crest of this ridge was wider, Ki loosed a sigh of relief, for his horse was breathing hard. A few dozen yards ahead, the ground spread out to form a flat-topped triangle that was virtually free from brush. Without reining in or looking for Steve, Ki started for the broad spot. When he reached it, the horse was still panting, and he swung out of the saddle to walk a few minutes and stretch his own legs while the animal rested.

Steve was still invisible when Ki looked around, and he walked leisurely toward the rim of the triangle to get a look at the valley between it and the next ridge. As he neared the dropoff and could gaze down into the valley, Ki's eyes widened with surprise and pleasure.

Along the eroded floor of the wide valley stood a string of shacks. The lumber they'd been built of glowed with newness. When he was within a few feet of the rim and could look almost directly down, long, heaped-up piles of freshly turned dirt told Ki that beyond any question he'd found the new mine Manfield was rumored to have started.

Ki began edging closer to the rim of the ledge to get a better look. He tensed instantly and bent his knees to spring backward in a *gedan-barai* turn, but the weight of his body and the downward thrust of his feet completed the work that natural erosion of the ledge had already started. The earth under his feet gave way and Ki plunged down with the falling clods. He somersaulted in midair to land on his feet, but a boulder that had been embedded in the dirt of the ledge bounced off his head.

Unconscious, Ki landed with a thud on the pile of dirt that stretched below the ledge, while the soil that was still falling from the collapsed ledge poured over him and covered him completely.

Chapter 11

As they started away from the mine, Lucy asked, "Are you sure we can prove that Mr. Manfield's a crook, Jessie?"

"No. But we can certainly try. However, I think we'd better get some advice on that."

"Who's going to advise us?" Lucy frowned. "We don't know anybody in Prescott."

"You're overlooking Mr. Cassidy, at the bank. He struck me as being very competent and honest. As soon as we get back to town, I'll pay him a call."

"But what about Steve and Ki? Shouldn't we find them and let them know what's going on? We might have to change some of the plans we've made."

Jessie gestured toward the brush and trees that lined the road. "We can't follow them in this kind of country, Lucy. As bad as this road is, the buggy couldn't get far if we turned off it, even if there was a chance that we'd be able to find them. Besides, we need to know what's going on, and if there's really another mine being started, Ki and Steve will find it. No, our only bet is to go back to town."

Jessie and Lucy talked very little during the remainder of their ride to Prescott. As they reached the town and started up Gurley Street, Lucy sighed and said, "I guess I'm not cut out for this wild sort of life, Jessie. I feel quite faint. Do I really need to go with you to call on Mr. Cassidy?"

Jessie realized belatedly that she'd been overlooking Lucy Chalmers's age, as well as the stress that her friend was under after her long trip. She glanced at Lucy and saw her face was indeed pale, and her hands were quivering nervously.

"We'd better go to the hotel without stopping at the bank," Jessie told Lucy. "I'll go up to your room with you, and help you into bed. Then I'll go to the bank and talk with Mr. Cassidy while you're lying down and resting."

"I'm sure I'll be all right after I've rested a little while."

Leaving the buggy at the hitchrail provided by the hotel for its patrons, Jessie made Lucy comfortable in her room, then walked the short distance to the bank. As she walked, she continued the inner debate that had occupied her mind during the ride back to town, and by the time she entered the bank she had reached a decision on the best way to proceed. Cassidy stood up when he saw her stop at the waist-high partition that divided his desk from the bank's lobby.

He smiled and nodded as he stopped at the partition and said, "Good afternoon, Miss Starbuck. Can I be of some further help to you today?"

"I'm sure you can," Jessie replied. "Since we talked yesterday, I've run into some rather upsetting details about the Empire mine, and I'd like to take advantage of your

124

offer to give me some additional advice—or, more accurately, some confidential information."

"Would you like to step back to my desk, then?"

"Oh, I don't think that's necessary. I'm looking for someone—some man—whom I can employ for a few days. He'd have to be someone who's totally trustworthy and not inclined to panic in an emergency, and who knows the area around Prescott."

"Well, that shouldn't be too difficult. I can think of two or three men whom I'd recommend. But if you care to be a little bit more specific—"

"Well, the man I'm looking for wouldn't be nervous or be bluffed easily. And he wouldn't be afraid to act in a— Well, let's say some distressing situation might arise when he might have to be very active."

"By 'distressing situation' and 'active,' I take it that you mean he might face physical violence?"

"I hope it doesn't come to that, but—yes, that's exactly what I mean, Mr. Cassidy."

"I hope you haven't run into serious trouble, Miss Starbuck, but from what you've just said—" Cassidy began.

Jessie interrupted him. "I hope there won't be anything really serious, but I wouldn't rule it out. I'm just not taking anything for granted."

"Well, in this part of the country right now, that's a very good attitude to adopt," Cassidy said, and nodded. "And what you've just said has helped me make up my mind. There's a young man here in Prescott whom I believe has a very bright future. He's bold, but not too impetuous. Just lately he's organized a local troop of volunteer militia, which he hopes to see become an auxiliary force to serve as volunteers to assist the local sheriff and police."

"He sounds like the sort of man I have in mind," Jessie agreed. "What sort of work is he doing now?"

125

"Right at the moment, he's without a job. I'm sure he'd like to have one, because I happen to know that he needs work."

"Then you can put me in touch with him?"

"Yes, of course."

"I don't think you've mentioned his name yet," Jessie said.

"William O'Neill, but everyone calls him Bucky. And I'll be glad to have him call on you. I think you said you're staying at the Burke Hotel?"

"Yes. You might mention that I'm willing to pay him quite adequately," Jessie added. "And that I'd expect him to work under not only my direction but also that of my assistant, who's here in Prescott with Mrs. Chalmers and me."

"I don't believe Bucky would object to that, Miss Starbuck, but I'll impress it on him. I suppose you'd like to talk with him as soon as possible?"

"I certainly would. Within the next few hours, if you can arrange it."

"That shouldn't be difficult," Cassidy said. "I know where he can be found most of the time. I think it's safe to say that he'll be calling on you within the next hour or two."

"Thank you, Mr. Cassidy," Jessie said. "Now, I'd better get back to the hotel and look in on my friend."

As Jessie left the bank and walked the short distance to the hotel, her mind was busy with plans. She went upstairs and tapped lightly at the door of Lucy's room. When there was no response, she tried the knob. The door opened readily, and she glanced inside. Lucy's bed was empty, its coverlet rumpled. Frowning, Jessie closed the door and walked down the corridor to the door marked LADIES' BATH. It, too, was unlocked, and when she looked inside it was as empty as Lucy's bedroom, the big white bathtub unoccupied.

Hurrying downstairs, she went to the desk and tapped the call button. "Yes, Miss Starbuck?" the clerk said as he stepped from behind the office partition. "What can I do for you?"

"I'm looking for Mrs. Chalmers," Jessie replied. "She's not in her room, and she wasn't feeling very well when we came in a half-hour or so ago. Do you happen to know whether she's gone out?"

"Why, yes," the clerk replied. "I saw her leave very soon after you did, escorted by a gentleman."

For a moment, Jessie felt something like panic seizing her, but she quickly pushed it aside. The years since Alex's death, when she'd had to meet so many emergencies, had taught her the necessity of keeping calm, no matter what the occasion.

"Did you know the gentleman Mrs. Chalmers was with?" she asked.

"I'm afraid I can't recall his name." The clerk frowned. "But I'm positive that I've seen him around town. Perhaps I even saw him here in the hotel, either in the lobby, or in our restaurant or our saloon."

"He wasn't one of the men traveling with us, then?" she persisted, thinking it possible that Ki and Steve had returned unexpectedly and that Lucy might have gone out with her stepson.

"Oh, no, indeed. If it had been the young Mr. Chalmers or your man Ki, I'd have recognized them. The gentleman who was with Mrs. Chalmers isn't a guest in the hotel."

"What did he look like? How was he dressed?"

"He was an older man than those in your party, Miss Starbuck," the clerk replied, his thoughtful frown reappearing. "I would say he was into his middle years, perhaps forty. He was rather heavily built, and clean-shaven. I remember noticing that his collar seemed somewhat too tight, and—now that you've reminded me—his suit was a plain brown serge, and it fitted him a bit too closely."

A tiny bell rang in Jessie's memory. Scanty as the clerk's description was, it recalled to her mind the man she and Lucy had seen come out of Manfield's offices at the mine. She nodded to the clerk.

"Thank you," she said. "You've been very helpful."

Certain now that Lucy was not in the hotel, and needing a moment of uninterrupted solitude to form a plan for finding and rescuing her, Jessie went upstairs to her room. She went first to her large portmanteau and took out the box of cartridges for her Colt, which she always carried while traveling. For the trip to the mine, she'd worn the gun in its soft leather cross-draw pouch sewn into the lining of her gabardine jacket, which snuggled the pistol inconspicuously into her left armpit.

Moving almost automatically, her mind occupied with quickly formed ideas which she discarded almost as soon as they formed, she began replacing the shells that had been in the Colt with loads fresh from the box. While Jessie's hands were busy, her mind was even busier, as she tried to think of a way to find Lucy and the man who'd taken her from the hotel. She'd made no progress in devising a plan when a tapping sounded at the door. She crossed the room and opened the door, still carrying the Colt in her hand.

A young man stood in the hall. He began to say "Would you be—" Then he saw the Colt Jessie was holding. Spreading his arms and holding his hands wide open he went on. "Ma'am, I'm not out to hurt anybody, and I'm not looking for trouble. I'm trying to find a lady named Miss Jessica Starbuck. My name's O'Neill."

128

Jessie lowered the Colt quickly as she replied, "I wasn't expecting you quite this soon, Mr. O'Neill. I'm Jessica Starbuck, and I'm very glad to see you. Please, come in."

Young O'Neill entered the room while Jessie took stock of him in quick flicking glances. She put his age as being in the middle twenties, and she noted the confident ease of his movements as he walked to the chair she'd indicated and settled into it.

Young O'Neill had taken off his flat-brimmed, peak-creased Stetson as he entered, revealing a high brow, thin eyebrows, and brown hair. His face was elongated by his narrow, pointed jaw, but his narrow, short-trimmed moustache broke its angular vertical lines and made less obvious the thin line of his lips. He had on a collarless shirt, its neckband open. His soft, flat-heeled stockman's boots shone with a fresh polishing job. Under his thigh-length coat the butt of a revolver bulged at his hip.

"Mr. Cassidy, down at the bank, said you needed somebody that knew the lay of the land here in Prescott to give you a hand," O'Neill said as Jessie pulled up a chair and sat down facing him. He indicated the box of cartridges open on the bed, glanced at the pistol that was still in Jessie's hand, and went on. "Looks to me like you got something real serious on your mind, if you're getting that Colt ready to use."

"I don't know how serious it is yet," Jessie replied. "But it's certainly very important to me."

"Mr. Cassidy didn't explain much about this job you've got open. He just told me you were looking for somebody to give you a hand," O'Neill said when Jessie fell silent. "Maybe you'd better tell me what you'd need me for if you hire me."

As they talked, Jessie had been studying O'Neill, and the calmness with which he'd met what could only be an unusual reception helped her to make a quick decision.

"I'm here from Texas with a very dear friend, one of my teachers from the school I attended in the East. Her son is with her and I brought my—" Jessie hesitated only a moment before falling back on the words she used to describe Ki's role to strangers, and went on—"my assistant from my ranch. My friend's husband left her a large block of stock in a gold mine near here, and she's concerned about its situation."

"That'd have to be the Empire." He nodded. "Seeing that it and the Iron King are the only gold mines left in this part of the territory that haven't petered out. Now, if it was the Iron King, you'd likely be staying closer to it, so that just leaves the Empire."

"You're right," Jessie agreed. His quick deduction and the manner in which young O'Neill spoke had settled any doubt left in Jessie's mind. "But this isn't the time to go into details about the mine. What's important is that we visited the Empire this morning to find out about some talk we'd heard regarding its condition after we got here. My friend—Mrs. Chalmers—came back to town with me while the men stayed to look around in the neighborhood of the mine. Then, after I left for the bank to talk to Mr. Cassidy, Mrs. Chalmers went somewhere with a man whose name and identity I don't know."

O'Neill was silent for a moment. Then he said, "Now, I don't mean to be nosey or pert, Miss Starbuck, but that sounds to me like it's just half a story. If you've got two men with you here, you're bound to be looking for some kind of trouble, or you wouldn't've gone to Mr. Cassidy and asked him to find somebody like me even before your lady friend got lost."

"You're right," Jessie agreed, more than ever convinced that she'd found the kind of man she was hoping to hire.

"There's quite a bit more that I'll need to tell you, but it'll have to wait. What I've got to do right now is find Mrs. Chalmers."

"You think she's in some kind of trouble?"

"I'm sure she is. When I asked about her at the desk, the clerk told me he'd seen her leave with a man, and I'm sure she didn't go willingly. From the sketchy description the clerk gave me of the man she left with, I suspect very strongly that he's the one Lucy and I saw when we were at the Empire mine this morning. His name is Rourke, and he says he's a lawyer. He visited Lucy here yesterday, trying to get her to sell him her stock in the mine."

"That'd be Donald Rourke, then." O'Neill nodded. "And he's a lawyer all right, but he's a long ways yet from making it up to the high-collar bunch."

"You mean you know him?"

"Well, Rourke and me don't drink at the same waterhole, Miss Starbuck, but this isn't all that big of a town." O'Neill smiled. "I guess everybody here just about knows everybody else. Sure, I know Donny Rourke. I got acquainted with him when he tried to join the Grays."

"I don't follow you," Jessie frowned.

"Oh, the Grays are a sorta militia outfit I got started here a while back. I tried to get into West Point, and I didn't have much luck, so I figured I'd do the next-best thing. But that's not here nor there, Miss Starbuck. You're worried about your friend right now, but there's got to be more to this job Mr. Cassidy said you had open than just finding her."

"There is." Jessie nodded. "But we'll talk about that later, after I'm sure Lucy's safe."

"Why, I'm not pushing to find out," O'Neill put in quickly when Jessie paused. "If you aim to hire me to help you, I'll be glad to take the job."

"Even without asking how much it'd pay?"

"Well, you look like a lady who'd give me a square deal." He smiled.

"Suppose you tell me what you call square," she suggested.

"A deputy sheriff here draws a dollar a day right now," O'Neill replied. "And the constable's deputy gets the same. I figure I ought to be worth that much."

"You'll be worth a great deal more, if you can really help me," Jessie replied. "Do you think you can?"

O'Neill nodded. "I've got a halfway idea. It popped into my mind the minute you'd finished telling me about your friend."

"You're already hired, Mr. O'Neill," Jessie said. "Now tell me what you plan to do to find my friend."

"I guess you've heard about Whiskey Row, even if you're new here in Prescott." When Jessie nodded, he went on. "Most everybody does, even if they've just got to town. And if you'll excuse my plain speaking, Miss Starbuck, everybody knows about the cribs behind it." O'Neill paused, but his eyes did not leave Jessie's face.

Realizing that he was awaiting her reaction, Jessie kept her expression unchanged. She nodded and said levelly, "I found out about Whiskey Row before I'd been in Prescott an hour. And I've seen cribs and parlor-houses in other towns. I'm not a bit bashful about plain talk. Go on."

"Well, now," O'Neill continued, "there's the red-light houses on the other side of Whiskey Row, and there's a few more houses of that sort scattered around town that don't show red lights in the window. They're the ones the muckety-mucks favor. Rourke's not up with the high-collar bunch yet, but he's trying real hard, and I just happen to know he hangs out with a woman in one of the houses that don't show a red light. If I was a betting man, I'd put up

132

money that's where he's got this lady you're so upset about. I guess you'd want me to go find out?"

"*We*, Mr. O'Neill," Jessie said quickly. "Because I'm going with you, wherever you think Lucy might be."

O'Neill was silent for a moment. Then he said, "I don't know how a man's supposed to act when he feels like he's got to talk back to a lady boss, Miss Starbuck. You see, you're the first one I've ever had. But I guess I better just spit out what's on my mind. That place I told you about's not one a lady like you ought to go into."

"There are very few kinds of places I haven't had to go into at one time or another," Jessie said, standing up. "I doubt that I'll see anything surprising. Now, let's get started."

Jessie gave her new employee credit for not arguing. O'Neill nodded and stood up. He stepped to the door and opened it for her to pass through. Jessie did not take time to lock the door, but started at once for the stairs, with O'Neill right behind her.

"How far is it to this place we're going?" Jessie asked as they hurried down the stairs.

"Not far; just to the next corner on Gurley Street and a street or two down Cortez."

They talked no more until O'Neill pointed to a two-story red brick house on the opposite side of the street. "That's Gracie Gold's place," he said. "And if my guess is right, we've got a pretty good chance of finding your friend inside."

"Will we have any trouble getting in?" she asked.

O'Neill did not answer for a moment. Then he said, "If I was by myself, there wouldn't be any. I don't know how Gracie's going to behave when she sees you with me."

"You might tell her I'm looking for work and asked you to bring me here," Jessie suggested. "Once the door's open, we'll try to get inside without making any sort of fuss that would attract attention. If we can't do that, you can just push the door open and we'll be on the inside. And after that—well, all we can do is take things as they come."

"You know, you're a real smart lady, Miss Starbuck," he replied, grinning. "That never occurred to me. Let's go, then."

Jessie took O'Neill's arm as they angled across the street and went up the low steps to the door. He knocked, and almost at once the door swung open. Against the shaded light of the hall beyond, daylight was not kind to the heavily made-up face of the tall blond woman who stood in the doorway.

"Howdy, Gracie," O'Neill said. "This lady asked me to show her where she could find you, so I obliged her."

"I heard about your place when I was down in Tombstone," Jessie said quickly. "And that town is dead, so here I am."

"Well—" Gracie said hesitantly. "I guess it won't do any harm to talk. You and Bucky come on in."

Chapter 12

Steve reined in when he came to the point where the ridge along which he'd been riding dipped sharply downward and merged with a long stretch of high-grassed mesa.

Though he did not know the peculiarities of the Western high country, he'd taken enough walking trips in the Poconos and the Green Mountains to understand how to read terrain. He looked back along the crest of the ridge and saw no sign of Ki, and decided that his best course was to follow the plan they'd agreed on. Tugging at the reins, he turned his horse and started north at right angles to the course he'd been following.

For a short distance ahead the low mesa stretched level and inviting, and for a mile or two Steve made rapid progress. Then he encountered a wide expanse of sawtooth ridges that changed the character of the land abruptly. He noted the first ridge that rose from the mesa on his left and passed it, passed the next ridge, and began looking for the third.

It was only a short distance away, and he turned the horse west. He reached another upslope within a few minutes and turned to follow it. As the ground rose sharply he kept looking for Ki, but until he'd been riding for a quarter of an hour there was no sign of his companion. Then he saw Ki's horse, standing motionless on the ridge he'd passed by earlier. But Ki was nowhere in sight.

"Now where on earth has Ki gone?" Steve frowned, muttering the question in the half-whisper used by men talking to themselves when alone. "He can't be too far away from his nag. Maybe he had to find a bush."

Frowning, Steve stood up in his stirrups to increase the range of his vision, as Jessie had taught him to do while they were riding across the Texas prairie. Even by adding such a small bit of elevation to his eyes he found that he could now see for some distance along the crest of the ridge beyond Ki's horse. He scanned the ridge carefully, but Ki was nowhere visible.

"There's bound to be something wrong, or I'd see him," Steve told himself. "And even if it's the wrong thing for me to do, I'd best go take a look."

Settling back into the saddle, he dug his heels into his horse's flank. Only a quarter-mile now separated him from the rise leading to the ridge where Ki's riderless horse still stood patiently. As he crossed the low oval-bottomed draw that marked the beginning of the canyon between the ridge he'd been supposed to follow and the one Ki was to cover, Steve kept his eyes busy scanning the landscape, but saw nothing moving. Even the horse toward which he was heading stood motionless.

Worry mounted in Steve's mind as more and more of the ridge ahead became visible. He could now see along the hump for more than a mile, and nothing was moving. Even the scanty leaves of the brittle greasewood clumps were motionless. As last he gained the crest, reined in beside Ki's horse, and looked down into the canyon. He gasped when he saw the line of shacks, but thrust them out of his mind when he noticed the fresh cracks in the soil at the canyon's rim.

Running to the drop-off, he looked down at the long piles of earth excavated by the miners, but Ki's unconscious body had been completely covered by the falling dirt. Belatedly, Steve noticed the difference between the light-colored dirt that had come from the mine and the darker reddish soil from the rim of the cliff. As his attention focused on the heaped-up earth directly below him, Steve could see Ki's unconscious form vaguely outlined on the pile of lighter-colored tailings.

"Oh, dear God!" he breathed, his words a prayer rather than an oath. "Ki must be buried in that pile of dirt, and he's almost sure to be unconscious or he'd be stirring up the dirt right now, trying to get out!"

"So you figured to change your luck by coming up here to Prescott from Tombstone?" Gracie asked as the door clicked shut and she turned to face Jessie. When Jessie merely nodded instead of speaking, Gracie went on, "You still haven't told me who it was down there that told you to try my place."

"It was one of the girls that worked in the same place I was," Jessie replied. She roughened her voice and reminded herself to fracture her grammar to fit the role she was playing. As she spoke, she wondered what Lucy Chalmers would say if she overheard her, after all the effort she'd spent teaching her to speak properly. "She was going by the name of Betty, but I ain't sure that's what it really was. Anyhow, she said you'd remember her."

As she spoke, Jessie was studying the other woman in the dim light of the emerald-shaped lamp that rested on the hall table. Even in the pinkish half-light that came through the pressed-glass, ruby-hued globe her sharp eyes quickly penetrated the heavy coating of powder and rouge and lip-salve that made a mask of Gracie's face.

Beneath the layers of makeup she could see the pebbling of the other woman's coarse skin, the cobwebbed maze of wrinkles at the outer corners of her eyes and the deep lines that ran from her thin nostrils to her lips, and told the surface story of her life. In spite of the time of day, Gracie had on a dress of watered silk, cut unusually low in the neck and fitted so snugly and pulled her over-full breasts together so tightly that they seemed to be spilling out of her bodice.

Gracie's frown had vanished, but now it flicked across her face again. "I know three or four Bettys," she said. "But none of them's in Tombstone. Now tell me what—" Her words ended in a strangled gulp as Jessie slid the Colt out and pressed its cold blue-steel muzzle into the cleft of Gracie's ballooning bosom.

"Stop worrying about Betty," Jessie said harshly. "I want to know where Donald Rourke and the lady he brought here are."

"You better tell her, Gracie," O'Neill put in. "You're in way deep—plumb over your head. This lady here can give you cards and spades and come up with high, low, Jack, and game."

"I don't know what you're talking about!" Gracie gasped.

"Stop lying and start talking!" Jessie snapped. "And don't try to shout and warn Rourke, if you know what's good for you!"

138

As she spoke, Jessie pulled back the hammer of her Colt. The snap of the steel sounded very loud in the quiet corridor. A gargled cry rose from Gracie's throat, but she strangled it and nodded.

"I'd sure as hell like to know how you found out that bastard brought her here!" she said. "But they're both upstairs, all right."

"Then you lead the way," Jessie commanded. "And if you try to yell and warn them, that'll be when I pull the trigger."

"Wait just a minute," O'Neill said. Turning to Gracie, he went on, "Before we take a step, you'd better give me that little pistol you've got in your garter. Hand it over, or I'll have to take it off of you myself."

"How do you know—" Gracie gasped, then stopped, her mouth open as though to shout.

O'Neill whipped his arm around and clamped his big muscular hand over Gracie's mouth. He said, "Don't play the fool, Gracie! Miss Starbuck might not pull the trigger, but *I* sure will if you make a sound! Now, do what I told you to! Hand over that little toy gun and keep quiet while you're doing it!"

Gracie managed a nod, and O'Neill removed his hand. She did not cry out, but with a garbled wheeze she strangled the cry that had been forming in her throat. Without taking her eyes off Jessie and O'Neill, Gracie pulled up her skirt and groped for a moment at her knee, then handed O'Neill the tiny .22-caliber revolver that she'd taken from her garter.

"All right," she went on. "I don't know how you tumbled to it, but they're upstairs, like I told you. Come on. I know when I'm beat. I won't raise no sort of ruckus."

With Jessie's Colt prodding her back, Gracie led the way through the dimly-lighted hall to the stairs. Thick carpeting smothered the sounds of their footsteps as Jessie and O'Neill followed her down the door-lined second-floor corridor. Stopping in front of the third door, she turned to them.

"They're in there," she said sullenly. "Now, are you satisfied?"

"Not quite yet," Jessie told her. Keeping her voice pitched low, she stepped behind Gracie and pressed the cold muzzle of her Colt into her bare back. Then she asked, "Rourke had you send a message to someone, or sent one himself, didn't he? And whisper when you answer me!"

Gracie hesitated for only a moment before nodding. "Yes. But I don't know who. He paid Flossie—she's one of my girls—ten dollars to carry a note to somebody."

"I was quite sure he'd done something like that," Jessie said. Then she hardened her voice and went on, "Now, knock on that door and tell him there's somebody here. Don't say anything else, or I'll put a bullet through you!"

Nodding obediently, Gracie tapped on the door. A man's muffled voice replied. Raising her voice, she called, "There's somebody here looking for you, Donny."

"All right," Rourke's muffled voice replied. "I'll be there in a minute."

In the instant before the doorknob rattled, Jessie shoved Grace to one side. Rourke opened the door. His jaw dropped when he saw Jessie. Then his hand moved toward his hip, and Jessie realized that she'd have no time to warn him not to draw.

Her finger tightened on the trigger of her Colt, but before she could squeeze off her shot O'Neill's pistol boomed. Rourke staggered back, then dropped in an ungainly sprawl to the floor.

* * *

Steve stood motionless for a moment, staring down at the lump in the pile of dirt. He was more positive than ever now that he could see Ki's supine form outlined under the off-color patch of earth that had drawn his attention. Then he suddenly became aware that he was wasting precious moments while Ki might be suffocating, and hurried to his horse.

Mounting, he backtracked to the head of the valley. Here, the floor of the cleft swept upward and narrowed to a point, and as he looked at the ragged nature of the terrain, Steve wondered if he had the skill to guide his mount into the gulch and onto its floor. Too concerned about Ki to waste time worrying and studying his problem, Steve set his jaw and kicked the animal's sides.

Luckily for him, the livery horse was more accustomed to the whims of strange riders than a range-horse might have been. It responded to the drumming of Steve's heels with a burst of speed, gained the momentum needed to span the short downward jump, and without breaking stride continued along the tiny crease to which the valley floor had dwindled at that point. The horse maintained its momentum as it danced in a zigzag along the valley floor, and in a matter of moments it had carried Steve to his destination.

Reining in, he dismounted quickly and began clawing with his bare hands at the tailings pile. The layer of dirt that covered Ki was dry and loose. It yielded readily to Steve's frantically pawing hands, and within a very short time his fingers encountered the fabric of Ki's loose jacket-like shirt. Feeling the cloth spurred Steve to greater effort. He locked his hands in the cloth, braced his legs on the shifting soil, and heaved. The layer of earth that still remained parted, and he was able to lift Ki free.

141

When he rolled Ki on his back, Steve saw that his eyes were closed and his face was smeared and flecked with grains of dirt. Kneeling beside Ki's supine form, he began brushing these away, trying to figure out what he could do to revive him. He'd cleared Ki's face of soil when Ki's chest heaved and his mouth and eyes opened. Gazing up at Steve, he blinked with surprise.

"Where did you come from?" he asked. "I saw you a minute or two before I fell, but you were back on the other ridge."

"I'd started to go to the next hump. Then I saw your horse, but I didn't see you, so I hurried over to find out what had happened."

"What happened was that I was careless and got too close to an undercut ledge on the rim," Ki replied. "I saw these mine tailings while I was up there, and I got off my horse to look at them more closely. Then the ground gave way, and that's all I remember." Sitting up, he looked at his surroundings and went on, "It seems we've found what we were looking for, and there don't seem to be any workmen around, or any guards. Let's take a closer look."

"Are you sure you're all right?"

"Of course I am!" Ki demonstrated his recovery by springing nimbly to his feet. He looked at the impression his body had made in the tailings pile and shook his head. "I was lucky. The dirt in that pile is so loose that it was almost like falling into a mattress, and I guess I gulped in enough air before I landed to keep me alive while you were getting here."

"What are we looking for?" Steve asked as Ki started toward the huts.

"I don't know, Steve," Ki replied. "But anything we can dig up about this place will be useful. From the looks of things here, the men I talked to at Chinese Gardens last

142

night were right. Manfield's started digging another mine shaft here, and I doubt that he'd go to all this trouble unless he was pretty sure of what he'd find."

"But there doesn't seem to be anybody around." Steve frowned. "Wouldn't there be a guard or a lookout?"

"Oh, I'd have one here, if I was in Manfield's place. But he may think that the fewer who know about what's going on, the better. Whatever the reason is, we seem to have free run of the place, so let's make the most of it."

They'd reached the first shack while they talked. The door was closed, secured by a simple hasp with a wooden peg securing the eye. Ki lifted out the peg and pushed the door open. A smell of old food and sweaty, unwashed bodies hit their nostrils. Steve coughed and halted just outside the door, but Ki had been in such places before and was prepared for the odor. He stepped into the shanty, and with a single sweep of his eyes took in the interior. Narrow bunks lined the walls, and a makeshift cobbled-up table occupied the center of the small room.

"Sleeping quarters for miners," Ki said over his shoulder as Steve came in to join him. "The men I talked to were right."

"Where are the miners?" Steve frowned. "Working?"

"Of course. And they must have some kind of boss, but I'd imagine that manpower's pretty short in the kind of mine they're digging."

"You seem to know a lot more about this place than I do, Ki." Steve frowned. "What kind of mine are you talking about?"

"An exploratory shaft," Ki replied. "I don't know as much as you think, though; and the little I do know isn't enough. Let's look some more."

When they moved along the line of jerry-built shanties, the first two they inspected were almost identical with the

143

first. The third shack was different. It lacked the overpowering smells of the others, and was furnished with a rusted iron bedstead, a sturdy table, a small potbellied stove, and three chairs. Shelves had been cobbled on one wall to hold crockery and cooking utensils. A stack of papers lay on the table, and Ki made a beeline for them. After he'd riffled through them quickly, he turned to Steve, who'd been exploring the bare-bones interior.

"They're digging for gold, all right," he said. "This is the log for the past few days."

"What does it show?" Steve asked eagerly. "Have they found gold here?"

"I haven't looked at it closely, Steve," Ki replied. "And I don't really know enough about gold mining to understand these papers without studying them for a while. But there'll be somebody in Prescott who does. We'll take them and get out of here as fast as we can. The most important thing we can do right now is to get this information to your mother and Jessie."

Ki and Steve were still bending over inspecting the documents when a man's harsh voice grated from the open doorway. "Just stand real still, you two! And put your guns on the table before you turn around! Then you can tell me who you are and what in hell you're doing prowling around here!"

"I think you've killed him!" Jessie said as she and O'Neill and Gracie stared at Rourke's motionless body.

"Yes, ma'am, that was the only thing I could do to keep him from shooting you," O'Neill replied.

"I understand that," Jessie nodded. "And—"

Lucy Chalmers broke in on Jessie to say, "I was wondering if you'd ever be able to find me, Jessie! That terrible man, the one your friend shot, he was going to take me

144

somewhere and keep me a prisoner until I agreed to sell my Empire mine stock. I just don't know what I'd have done if you and the gentleman who shot this person hadn't gotten here when you did."

"I'm real sorry I had to shoot to kill, ma'am," O'Neill told Lucy. "But if I hadn't, Miss Starbuck would likely have been a goner."

"I'm just grateful that you shot fast," Jessie broke in to say.

"Well, I sure as hell ain't!" Gracie exploded. "It won't help my place one bit when the word gets around that somebody got killed in here! Bucky O'Neill, what gives you the right—"

"Mr. O'Neill has the same right any citizen has to intervene on the side of the law when a crime is being committed," Jessie told the bawdyhouse madam.

Gracie was silent for a moment while she eyed Jessie. Then she said, "You had me fooled for a while, but now I want to know just who in hell you are, lady. Because you sure ain't no hooker looking for a place to turn your tricks."

"My name is Jessica Starbuck," Jessie replied. "And it certainly wasn't my idea to bring my friend here. Blame your troubles on yourself for letting that man use your—your place as a hideout while he was committing a crime!"

"It's not as bad as it could be, Gracie," O'Neill said. "I imagine between the strings you and Miss Starbuck can pull, you won't be hurt very bad. But the law says I've got to report this shooting to the sheriff and turn myself in, so that's what I'm aiming to do just as quick as Miss Starbuck figures out what her next move's going to be."

"It seems to me the first thing we'd better do is get Lucy back to the hotel and call a doctor to look at her," Jessie told him. "Then I suppose the sheriff will be around to ask all of us some questions, but I haven't had time to plan anything. Finding Lucy has kept me too busy."

"What about me?" Gracie put in. "Here I got a dead man in one of my rooms, and evening's coming on. A lady's got a right to make a living, but I don't see a dime coming in tonight!"

"I'm sure you'll recover your losses quickly when news of the shooting gets around," Jessie told the madam.

"You know, I think you're right," Gracie said, a smile beginning to form on her raddled face. She turned to O'Neill and went on, "Get your business with the sheriff finished as fast as you can, Bucky. It's getting later every minute, and I've got to see that this room's cleaned up so I won't have to keep too many johns waiting in the parlor tonight!"

"Don't worry," O'Neill replied. "I'll walk over to see him as soon as I get Miss Starbuck and her friend back safe to the hotel. I'll even do you a favor without you asking me—I'll stop by the undertaker's and tell him you'll be needing some service as soon as the sheriff's finished."

"Don't put yourself out on my account!" Gracie snapped. She turned to Jessie and went on, "Or you, either, miss! Just get out of my place as fast as you can! I run a respectable whorehouse, and what you've done's not going to help me a bit!"

As Jessie and O'Neill, supporting Lucy between them, got to the door of the hotel, Jessie said, "You'd better go and make that report you mentioned."

"Yes, ma'am." O'Neill nodded. "I sure wouldn't want you to get into trouble on my account."

"Nonsense!" Jessie exclaimed. "As far as I'm concerned, you're working for me now, and I'll take care of any problems that might come up."

146

"There won't be anything said, Miss Starbuck. You and this lady both saw that Rourke drew first and was about to shoot me when I drew."

"Well, when you're through at the sheriff's office, come back to the hotel. Ki and Steve should be getting in from the mine very soon. I haven't any idea what they've found, and they may not have turned up anything at all, but regardless of that, we'll have to plan our next move. This business seems to've gained momentum, and I want to push it to a finish just as fast as possible. Then Lucy and Steve can go on with their trip, and Ki and I can go back to the Circle Star and pick up our own affairs."

Chapter 13

"We have no guns," Ki told the man in the doorway. "You can search us if you don't believe me."

"What the hell are you doing messing around here?" The man frowned. He did not lower the muzzle of his weapon. "This is private property, and you got no business poking around it."

"But we didn't know that!" Ki insisted.

He was sizing the man up as he spoke. The newcomer's jaws were blackened, masked with the beginning of a beard. A jagged scar ran down one cheek, and his red-rimmed eyes were slitted in anger. Saddlebags hung over one shoulder and in addition to the rifle in his hands he was armed with a pistol in a gunbelt. The belt was worn low, the sign of a gunfighter.

Ki went on, marshalling his thoughts as he spoke. "We were just riding around to take a look at the countryside, and happened to stumble on this place."

For the first time the man noticed the sheaf of papers Steve was holding. His scowl deepened and he asked, "What're you doing messing around with them papers? They don't belong to you! Put 'em back where you found 'em!"

"We saw them on the table and just picked them up to look at them," Steve answered, replacing the sheaf of documents on the table. "Neither of us could make heads or tails of them."

"Just as well you couldn't!" the man with the rifle growled angrily. He went on, "You told me you was out for a ride. If that's so, where's your horses?"

"Up at the end of the canyon," Ki replied. "There wasn't anybody around, and we thought it was an old deserted mine."

"Well, it ain't! Like I said, it's private property, and the boss don't want nobody messing around on it." He frowned and asked, "How in hell did you get here, anyhow? There's supposed to be a guard on the trail. How'd you get by him?"

"We didn't see any guard," Steve said quickly. "Like my friend told you, we were just out for a ride."

"Damned if you two don't talk funny!" the man exclaimed. "You ain't from around here. Where'd you come from?"

"Prescott. We are visiting there." Ki could see that their hastily concocted story was convincing the man with the rifle. "My friend here is from the East; I live in Texas."

For a moment the man with the rifle stood scowling. Then his menacing expression faded. He said, "Well, you can just get your tails outta here, but I'll walk up the canyon with you and make sure you ain't been spinning me a yarn."

"Whatever you say." Ki nodded. Anything that would

149

lull the guard's suspicion would work to their advantage, and he had no intention of leaving without the sheaf of documents that Steve had replaced on the table. He started toward the man.

"If your horses are up the canyon, like you say," the guard went on, "you can ride back to wherever you started, as long as you keep your traps shut about this place. If some of them damn burro-prospectors in Prescott finds out we've hit a good strike here, they'd pile out and play hell with our job."

Ki was within striking distance of the man now. He brought up his leg in a *mai-geri* kick that caught the barrel of the rifle and sent it spinning through the air.

As the weapon fell from the guard's hands and sailed through the air, Ki twirled and bent from his waist, carrying the kick onward to make it a *jodan* strike. His target was now the man's jaw, and his foot met it with a solid *thwack*. The rifle slid from the guard's hands as he sagged, and his eyes fluttered before closing while he lurched sidewise and then collapsed, his prone body stretching half inside and half outside the doorway.

He'd made a half-turn while he was falling, and as he hit the floor the saddlebags fell from his shoulder and dropped beside him with a heavy thud. Their flaps had not been buckled, and a half-dozen small leather bags popped out onto the floor.

"Will he be unconscious long enough for us to get away?" Steve asked.

"Of course he will," Ki replied. He was eyeing the sacks that had spewed from the saddlebags. "But we've got to gather up those sacks and take them with us."

"Why? What's in them?"

"That's the kind of sacks miners use to carry ore samples to the assay office," Ki explained. As he spoke he was scooping up the sacks and returning them to the saddle-bags. "And this fellow must've been coming in to get the reports to go with them. Grab those papers on the table and let's go! He'll be out of action long enough for us to get away!"

"But if he does come to, he'll start after us with that rifle—" Steve began.

"I'll put it out of commission!" Ki broke in. "You take care of the papers. I'll hold on to the saddlebags while I disable his rifle!"

Steve moved back to the table and began straightening out the scattered reports. Ki picked up the rifle and jammed its muzzle into the soft dusty ground outside the door. He triggered the weapon. Its muffled report sounded, the barrel tried to force itself from the ground. A bulge formed in the barrel, the forestock splintered, and the ejector cracked and popped out of its grooves. Leaving the now useless weapon sticking up like a truncated hitching-post, Ki yanked the prone guard's revolver from its holster and handed Steve the weapon as they started running up the canyon.

"I know that Jessie was teaching you how to use a pistol before we left the Circle Star," he said. "Take this. I have my *shuriken*, but if that fellow gets some of the miners together and starts chasing us when he comes to, this gun might come in handy."

"Ki, I've never shot at anybody in my life!" Steve panted.

"Just remember what you've learned from Jessie," Ki said. "And it doesn't matter whether you hit him or not; the noise ought to slow him down."

Running side by side, Ki and Steve reached the end of the canyon. Steve's horse was still standing where he'd left it.

"Start for the ridge," Ki said. "I'll be up there and on my horse by the time you get to me."

As Steve swung into his saddle, Ki began clambering up the steep slope to the ridge. In spite of the heavy saddle-bags and the shifting soil that gave way under the pressure of his feet, he made it to the top and was mounting his horse by the time Steve rode up.

"We'll be heading back to town, I suppose?" he asked Ki.

"Certainly. Jessie will be wondering what's happened to us. We should have been back long before now."

"What about that fellow down in the canyon?"

"More than likely he'll make a beeline for the Empire, to tell Manfield what's happened," Ki replied as he nudged his horse into motion. "But if we cut cross-country and head directly for Prescott, we'll beat him there, and Jessie will know what we've stumbled onto out here. Now, let's ride!"

"I think you'd better lie down, Lucy," Jessie said as they entered Lucy's room at the hotel. "You've had enough excitement for one day, and you need to rest awhile until you're over the shocks you've had."

"I don't think so many things have ever happened to me in such a short time before," Lucy sighed. "My goodness! To think that I saw a man shot to death right in front of my eyes! And in a house of ill repute, at that! I suppose the West is just as wild as I've always heard it was."

"That sort of thing doesn't happen often," Jessie assured her friend as she slipped Lucy's shoes off and drew the bedspread up to cover her. "I'll stay here with you, but first I'd better go down to the desk and leave word for Ki and Mr. O'Neill, so they'll know where to find us. Now you just relax. I'll be right back."

152

When Jessie returned, Lucy was sleeping soundly. Jessie sat down in one of the armchairs, leaned back, and closed her own eyes, taking for herself the advice she'd given Lucy. She had no idea how long she'd been dozing when a knock at the door roused her. O'Neill stood in the doorway when she opened the door.

"Hope I didn't disturb you and your friend, Miss Starbuck," he apologized. "But you said you wanted me to come back here."

"Yes, of course." Jessie nodded. "But suppose we step down the hall to my room to talk. Mrs. Chalmers is sleeping."

When they were comfortably seated in Jessie's room, she said, "It didn't take you very long to settle things at the sheriff's office."

"No, ma'am. A shooting's not such a much hereabouts. They said if you and your friend and Gracie backs up what I told them had happened, they wouldn't file charges against me."

"They just let you walk away?"

"Why, they know I'm not going anywhere, Miss Jessie. This town's where I live. Besides, there's a lot of Grays that belong to the sheriff's posse; and so do I, for that matter, even if the sheriff knows I've sorta got my eye on his job."

"I don't know the sheriff, but you've proven yourself to me today, Mr. O'Neill, and I wish you well. But you've mentioned the Grays before. What exactly are you talking about?"

"Oh, it's kind of a militia outfit that I started. There's a lot of war veterans that came West after Appomattox, you know, and they gave me the idea. We wear gray uniforms because most of the men hereabouts fought under the Stars and Bars."

153

"I see." Jessie nodded. "And you're what, the captain?"

"They picked me out for the job," O'Neill replied. "So if those fellows out at the Empire mine act too rough, I can get a pretty good bunch together to take your side, Miss Starbuck."

"I hope that won't be necessary," Jessie said. "But just the same, I appreciate your offer. As for the mine, I suppose now's as good a time as any to explain that situation to you."

"It'd be right helpful, ma'am. You said you figured there was some kind of dirty work going on out there, but there wasn't time to go into all of it."

Briefly, and omitting much background detail, Jessie sketched Lucy's problem and the few steps they'd taken to date. She concluded by saying, "You saw for yourself just a couple of hours ago how far Manfield is ready to go. And I don't propose to let him get away with it."

"As far as I'm concerned, a crook's a crook," O'Neill told her. "But where do I fit in?"

"Ki and I can take care of ourselves," Jessie answered. "But Lucy and Steve— Well, they're Easterners who're used to stepping to the corner to call a policeman. I want you to keep an eye on Lucy especially, because she'd be the main target if Manfield decides to get rough."

"Sort of a bodyguard, then?"

"That's about as close to it as I can come." She nodded. "Will you take the job, Mr. O'Neill?"

"Why, I'd be proud to, Miss Starbuck. But—well, I don't answer to 'mister' so good. Would you and your friends mind just calling me Bucky?"

"Not a bit. And I don't object at all when friends call me Jessie."

"It seems like to me that things are friendlier when folks don't have to put on a show of being polite," Bucky

O'Neill went on. "Now, if you've worked out what you'll want me to do next, I'll get started on it right away."

"Until Ki and Steve get back from their scouting trip, there isn't a great deal any of us can do," Jessie said. "But while we're talking about doing things, there's something I've decided to do immediately."

"What's that, Jessie?"

"Increase your salary or fee. Your services are certainly going to be worth much more than the figure we discussed. I think ten dollars a day would come closer to being fair. If you need an advance, I'll be glad to pay you for a week right now."

"Well, I'm what you'd call not hurting for money right now, Jessie," Bucky told her. "But I do appreciate you boosting my pay."

"Don't think you won't earn it," Jessie smiled. "Lucy's kidnapping is just the beginning. And I'm sure we'll have more to do when—"

A light tapping at the door interrupted Jessie. She stood up and opened it. Ki and Steve were standing in the corridor.

"We've been wondering what happened to you," Jessie said. "Come on in and tell us."

Ki and Steve came in. Both stopped short when they saw Bucky O'Neill getting up from the chair in which he'd been sitting. Jessie said quickly, "This is Bucky O'Neill, Ki. While you and Steve were scouting out at the mine, Manfield's crony kidnapped Lucy. She's—"

"Kidnapped her!" Steve exclaimed. "Hadn't we better—"

Jessie interrupted him. "Don't worry, Steve," she said.

"Hadn't I better go see how she is?" Steve asked.

"She was in her room sleeping soundly when I looked in

on her just a few minutes ago," Jessie replied. "And that's the best thing she can do."

"I'm sorry I wasn't here when you needed me, Jessie," Ki said. "But we didn't have any way—"

"Of course you didn't," Jessie said. "But since I had no idea when you and Steve would be back, I needed to move quickly. I don't know anything about Prescott, so I went to the bank and asked Mr. Cassidy to recommend someone who did. He sent Mr. O'Neill to help me, and very quickly he found out where Lucy was. Once we knew that, we went and got her with only a little bit of trouble." She turned to O'Neill and said, "I've told you about Ki and Steve, Bucky. Now here they are."

"And I'm right glad to meet you men," O'Neill said quickly. He stepped forward to shake hands with Ki and then with Steve. "I didn't rightly know who Jessie was talking about before."

Ki turned back to Jessie and said, "You mentioned having a little trouble. Was it—"

"Maybe I understated a bit, Ki," Jessie broke in. "I missed not having you with me, but Bucky was about as good a substitute as I could've hoped for."

Ki contented himself with a nod. He and Jessie had shared so many perilous encounters in the past, together as well as apart, that he felt no rancor toward Bucky O'Neill. He turned to Bucky and said, "Thank you, Mr. O'Neill. You must have done very well for Jessie to compliment you so highly."

"Make it Bucky, if you don't mind, Mr. Ki. And Jessie might change her mind about hiring me, now that you're back. I sure don't want to butt in and jar things up any."

"Do not worry," Ki replied. "Prescott is strange to both Jessie and me. If she has decided that we need help, I agree with her fully."

156

Steve broke into their conversation. He said to O'Neill, "Jessie mentioned that you'd had some trouble. Mother wasn't harmed, was she?"

"Of course not, Steve," Jessie said before Bucky could answer. "But Bucky had to shoot the man who'd kidnapped Lucy. I'm sure that the man was in cahoots with Manfield, because he was the one who tried to buy Lucy's Empire mine stock."

"How can you be sure?" Steve asked.

"Lucy and I saw him coming out of Manfield's office when we went there after you left us to go scouting," Jessie told him. "And speaking of that, I see you've brought back a pretty good load from wherever you went. Now, let's sit down and be comfortable while you and Ki tell me what you've found."

"If you folks want to talk private," O'Neill broke in, "I can leave and come back tomorrow."

Jessie shook her head. "You'd better stay and hear what Ki and Steve have to say, and what they brought back from their scouting trip today." She turned to Ki and went on, "Go ahead, Ki. I know from the dirt on your clothes that you must've gotten into some kind of scrape, and I'm anxious to find out what's in those saddlebags."

Condensing his story as much as possible, Ki concentrated on relating the evidence he and Steven had discovered that indicated new and hidden mining operations in the isolated canyon, and the encounter they'd had with the man who'd had the ore samples.

"We didn't waste any more time looking around, once we'd gotten our hands on those reports and samples," he concluded. "We just started back here as fast as we could ride."

"I'm certain you've stumbled onto some of Manfield's crooked work!" Jessie exclaimed after Ki had finished.

"Steve and I were sure it is, too," Ki agreed. He turned to Bucky and went on, "You know this area better than any of us do. Have you heard of anyone starting to put down a new mine?"

O'Neill shook his head. "Not even a whisper," he replied. "And in this town the word of a new strike or a new mine would spread like wildfire."

"I imagine you'd be sure to've heard about it, even if it was just a rumor?" Ki asked.

"I sure would if it was a new outfit at work," Bucky replied. "But somebody in Manfield's place wouldn't have too much trouble putting down a new shaft. All he'd have to do would be switch some of his regular crew to wherever he'd want 'em to dig. If it was me setting about on a job like that, I'd do what I figure is going on from what you just told us about, Ki. I'd keep my miners out of town and not let anybody come poking around."

"Then those ore samples you and Steve brought back must be from the new shaft, Ki." Jessie frowned.

Ki nodded. "Assay samples. I knew when I saw them that's all they could be."

Jessie turned to O'Neill. "Is there an assay office in Prescott?"

"Not anymore," he answered. "There used to be three or four of 'em here, before all the little mines petered out, and when prospectors were swarming all over the hills. But the last one closed down about two years ago."

"Where would Manfield have to send those samples to be assayed, then?" she asked.

"To the Iron King," O'Neill replied promptly. "That's where he sends the Empire ore to be smelted, and it's the only place closer than Tombstone where there's an assay office."

"How far is the Iron King?" Jessie went on.

158

"Oh, right at twenty miles, if you push pretty good."

"We'd better take those samples there tomorrow, then, Ki," Jessie said decisively. She went on, "Bucky can stay here and make sure that Lucy won't be harmed again."

Steve spoke up. "Much as I'd like to go with you and Ki and get a look at a real Western gold mine, Jessie, I think I'd better stay here with Mother, too."

"Yes," Jessie agreed, "because Ki and I will be riding hard, and you're still learning about the kind of riding we'll be doing."

O'Neill stood up. "It doesn't look like you'll be needing me anymore this evening, Jessie, but if you want me to stay, I'll be glad to. All I've got on hand tonight is a drilling exercise with the Grays, but the lieutenant can handle that as well as I can."

"Go ahead, by all means," Jessie said. "And I'd appreciate it if you'll come to the hotel early in the morning, because Ki and I will be leaving as soon as there's enough light to see."

After O'Neill had gone, Ki turned to Jessie and asked, "Do you think Lucy's rested enough to go to dinner outside of the hotel? Because I'd like to visit my friend Chijin Yamata and find out what he's heard since yesterday."

"Oriental food?" Jessie smiled. "I'd enjoy it." She turned to Steve. "Would you go ask Lucy if she feels like going out? I know that if Ki takes us to his friend's restaurant we'll be treated like royalty, and after what's happened today, I rather think she'd enjoy it."

★

Chapter 14

"I'd say that you made a wise choice when you hired young O'Neill, Jessie," Ki commented after Chijin Yamata had left the table to carry their dinner orders to the kitchen. "He seems to be a very competent young man."

"Courteous, too," Lucy broke in before Jessie could speak. "I was afraid of him after I saw him shoot that terrible man who took me to that awful place and threatened to kill me, but now I've changed my mind about him."

"He certainly seems to know where to look for crooks here in Prescott," Steve said. "If he could find Mother in such a short time, he's bound to be pretty smart."

"Don't give me any credit for selecting Bucky O'Neill," Jessie told her companions. "Mr. Cassidy sent him to me, and I hired him not only because of his recommendation, but because time was so short that I didn't have any other choices."

Their table-talk stopped when Chijin returned. In one hand he carried a tray bearing four small delicate porcelain cups without handles, and in the other a large teapot with steam rising from the spout.

"A sip of *Mook Li Far* will make time pass more pleasantly while you are waiting for your dinner," he said. After he'd placed the teapot and cups on the table, he turned to Ki. "If I may ask the indulgence of your companions, Ki, I would like to speak with you privately for a moment."

"Of course." Ki nodded, stood up, and followed Chijin to a corner several feet distant from the table.

"One of my friends—not one you talked with at the Gardens, but another, has given me some disquieting news," Chijin said, his voice pitched low.

"Disquieting to us, I suppose, or you would not be telling me," Ki suggested.

Chijin nodded and continued, "My friend Lin runs the fan-tan parlor a few doors from here. He is also *kobu-do*, and we have few secrets from one another. The day before yesterday he was visited by a man who is not of good repute, and was asked by him to provide someone who has great skill in *do*, and who will sell his skill to others."

"Did he say why he wants such a man?"

"No. But he could have only one reason, Ki. You are Miss Starbuck's protector. Alone, she would be very vulnerable."

Ki smiled. "Don't underestimate Jessie. She can hold her own against almost anybody."

"But if you were to be kept from helping her by a *do* who could match your skill, and other men at the same time were to set on her, there could be great danger to both of you."

Ki had already realized that. He nodded and asked, "This man who wanted the *do*, was he of our people?"

Chijin shook his head. "He has a saloon on Whiskey Row. He is not a good man, Ki. He provides hiding places for men wanted by the law."

"And other services, too, I imagine?"

"So I have heard."

"Can he find a man such as he wants here in Prescott?"

Chijin shook his head. "No. In all of Arizona Territory there are only two. One is in Tucson, the other in Tombstone."

"If the man should locate one of them without the help of your friend Lin, how long would it take for him to get here?"

"Two days, if the matter was arranged by telegrams."

"He could be here today, if he left at once," Ki said thoughtfully. "Or perhaps no later than tomorrow."

"That is the thought that occurred to me," Chijin replied.

"Then I will be on guard." Ki nodded. "Thank you for telling me, Chijin."

Jessie opened the door to Ki's soft tapping after they'd returned from supper and settled down in their own rooms. Hiding her surprise when she saw her caller was not Steve, she swung the door open, and Ki slipped in.

"I didn't want to alarm Lucy and Steve by mentioning this at supper," he said. "When Chijin took me aside this evening, it was to warn me that someone here in Prescott is trying to find an Oriental combat master to bring into town."

"You'd be his target, of course," Jessie said calmly.

Ki nodded. There were no surprises that could rattle either of them, after years of battling the array of killers of every description that the cartel had sent to eliminate them.

"When is this man supposed to get to Prescott?" Jessie asked, her voice still level, almost casual.

"He may be here now, he may arrive tomorrow," Ki replied. "Certainly not later than the following day. I was wondering if you think we should delay our trip to the Iron King, or if we should take Lucy and Steve with us."

Jessie needed only a moment to make a decision. "Neither," she said firmly. "Bucky O'Neill will be here early tomorrow morning. He'll keep an eye on Lucy and Steve. We'll start as soon as he gets here and go to the assay office, just as we'd planned."

"Yes, of course," Ki said. "When will Bucky get here?"

"I invited him for breakfast, and he said he'd be here but might be a bit late. He had some personal business to take care of, something to do with his Prescott Grays, I suppose. But we needn't leave too early, Ki. Regardless of what time we get to the Iron King, we'll have to stay overnight. I understand they have accommodations for visitors in the compound they maintain for their workers."

"Is it safe to leave Lucy and Steve for two days, Jessie?"

"Of course. Bucky can stay here overnight, to be on hand in case there's trouble. And we must have that ore from the new mine assayed, Ki. If Manfield's made a big strike on land that's part of the Empire's property, it'll certainly solve Lucy's problems."

"I can see that," Ki agreed. "I'll let you go to bed, then, and get some sleep myself."

Walking down the corridor to his room, Ki went in. He took off his loose black vest and tossed it on a chair. Then he removed his *shuriken* from the pocket he carried them in. He was placing them on the table when a thought struck him.

Picking up one of the thin, carefully tempered six-pointed throwing blades, he held it close to the lamp and

163

looked at it closely. The needle-sharp points and keenly-honed, razor-sharp edges of the blades threw sparkling glints back into his eyes as he turned it in the lamplight. He studied the blade for several moments, then returned it to the pocket of his vest. Putting the vest back on, he went downstairs to the reception desk and tapped the call-bell.

A sleepy-eyed clerk came from behind the partition, looked at Ki, and asked, "Yes, sir. How can I be of service?"

"You can tell me where to find the best blacksmith's shop in town," Ki replied.

"That won't be hard. There are only two left in Prescott now, and from what I understand they're both quite good. But I'm afraid they're both closed now. Perhaps tomorrow—"

Ki broke in, "That's not going to help me. I need a good blacksmith tonight."

"Well, there's the shop that belongs to the hotel. We keep a man on duty all night; so many of our guests come in with a horse that's thrown a shoe on these rough roads, or with a carriage that needs repairs. Perhaps the night man can help you. The shop's right around the corner on the side street, across from our carriage entrance."

Ki went around the corner and found the blacksmith's shop's big double-door closed. But light showed around its edges. He tapped, lightly at first, then more vigorously, until a man's voice sounded inside.

"Hold on to your horses!" the man said. "I'm gittin' there fast as I can." One of the doors swung open a foot or two, and an old man, stooped with age, looked at Ki, then beyond him. He frowned and said, "I don't see no horse. You staying at the Burke Hotel, mister? Because if you ain't, I can't do no work for you. This here's a private smithy."

164

"I know that," Ki replied. "And I am staying at the Burke. It was the desk clerk who suggested that I come here."

"Well, where's your horse? Or your carriage or wagon or buggy or whatever it is that needs a smith to fix up?"

"I don't have a horse or carriage or anything else that needs repairing," Ki replied. "I'm looking for a blacksmith who knows his trade well enough to do a special job, a delicate job. Is there a smith like that in Prescott?"

"Hell, mister, there ain't but two smithies left in this town, now that the prospectors have raked over the country and moved on without finding much. But if you're staying at the hotel and need some special work on your buggy or saddle gear, I kin do fine work, or useta could."

"What do you call fine work?"

"Well, when I was blacksmithing in San Francisco, before the doctor said I had to git outta all that fog and rain and come someplace like here, where it's high and dry, I used to work in a shipyard that belonged to a Mr. Alex Starbuck, and—"

"Wait a minute!" Ki exclaimed. "I knew there was something familiar about you! You're Joab Peters!"

Peering carefully at Ki's face, the oldster asked, "Are you Ki? The fellow Mr. Starbuck—damned if you ain't! But you was a lot younger, then, just like I was! Come on inside here, Ki! I don't know what you want a blacksmith to make at this time of night, but I can sure bust my britches trying!"

"I'm wondering what's happened to Ki," Jessie told Lucy and Steve as they met in the hallway outside their rooms. "I've knocked on his door, but he doesn't answer. It's not like him to fail to tell me when he's going to be gone very long, but I suppose he's making sure that our horses will be

165

ready, or getting something we'll need for our trip. We won't wait for him, though. Bucky's supposed to meet us for breakfast, so let's go down to the restaurant. Ki will find us when he gets back."

Jessie and the others had almost finished breakfast when O'Neill came into the hotel dining-room. He saw them at the big round table, where empty chairs waited for him and Ki, and he hurried to join them.

"I'm sorry if I'm late," he told Jessie after they'd exchanged greetings. "But I see I'm not the only one missing. I imagine Ki will be here soon, though."

"Yes, of course," Jessie said. "He's out doing some early-morning errand, I'm sure. But sit down, Bucky. We really don't have too much to talk about; you know what you'll be doing while Ki and I are gone."

"I sure do," O'Neill replied. "Keep Mrs. Chalmers and Steve from getting hurt by anybody else Manfield might send out to get them."

Jessie nodded, then turned to Lucy and Steve. "Please stay close to Bucky," she said. "Don't either of you go out of the hotel unless he's with you."

"I'm certainly not going anywhere," Lucy told her. "In fact, I think I'll go back up to my room right now. I'm still a bit tired from yesterday."

"Then I'll go with you," Steve volunteered. "I can use a little more rest myself after the wild ride Ki and I had yesterday. The riding I did on the Circle Star didn't prepare me for anything like that."

After Lucy and Steve left, Jessie said to O'Neill, "There is one thing I'd like you to help me with. I understand the road to the Iron King gold mine is a bit difficult to follow, and I'd like you to give me any directions we might need."

"It's not a hard road to follow if you keep on the tracks left by the Empire's ore wagons," O'Neill replied. "But it does twist around a lot, because those wagons have to follow the easiest grades when they're hauling a load of ore down there to the smelter. You can save a lot of miles by cutting across the curves on the old road when you're on horseback."

"I suppose there are landmarks we should be looking for to avoid the twists and turns?" She frowned.

"Sure there are," O'Neill replied. "I'll get that waiter to bring us some paper, and I'll make a few hen-scratches for you."

For a moment or two, O'Neill busied himself drawing lines and jotting notes on the hotel stationery the waiter provided. Then he placed his work in front of Jessie.

"You go out of town on Gurley Street till it turns into the old army road to Fort Whipple," he said. "Just about the time you get close enough to see the barracks there's a road that'll branch off to the southeast. It'll take you into Kirquil Valley, and doesn't have any turn-offs until you see some buildings off to the right. That'll be Peeples's place. Turn east on the next spur off the road, and you'll wind through Antelope Valley on an easy downgrade until you see the mine smelter's stack. That's all there is to it."

"It sounds simple enough." Jessie nodded. "And I'm sure we won't have any problems."

She saw Ki making his way toward the table, and a small frown rippled across her brow. Ki wore his regular black blouse, vest, and trousers, and the narrow white scarf that bound his coarse black hair. But he also wore a second scarf around his neck, looped into a loose fold at his throat.

Jessie went on, "Here's Ki now. If he's had breakfast, we'll be leaving right away."

"I'm sorry I wasn't here in time to join you at breakfast, Jessie," Ki said as he reached the table. He nodded a good morning to O'Neill and went on, "But I had a few little

167

things to look after. I ate early, then went to get our horses ready."

"We were wondering what happened to you," Jessie said. She was looking at Ki as she spoke, and a small frown formed on her face; somehow his appearance seemed to be changed a bit. Deciding that the dim light of the dining-room was playing tricks on her eyes, she went on. "I was pretty sure you'd gone to get the horses saddled, though. Are we ready to leave, then?"

"As soon as I get my saddlebags," Ki said. "If you'll give me the key to your room, I'll bring yours down too, and save you from walking upstairs."

Jessie passed the key over and watched Ki as he wove between the tables toward the dining-room door. She turned to O'Neill and asked, "Does Ki look any different to you, Bucky?"

O'Neill shook his head. "I can't say he does, Jessie. Why?"

"I don't know," she replied, speaking slowly and thoughtfully, keeping her eyes on Ki's back until he disappeared through the door. "But there's something that bothers me about his appearance. I can't say what it is, but it's there."

"Maybe it's the light in this room," O'Neill suggested. "It doesn't have any windows. I like sunlight, myself. It throws good, honest shadows and you can see everything sharp and clear."

"You're probably right," Jessie said. "It's either the light or my imagination." She stood up. "I hope you don't have any trouble while we're gone. Lucy and Steve still don't realize that the West isn't tame and placid the way New England is. But I'm not going to worry. As long as you're with them, I'll know they're safe."

"They'll stay safe, if I have anything to do with it," he

168

promised as they stopped at the foot of the stairway to wait for Ki. "And you can bank on it."

"I don't have a bit of doubt about that," Jessie replied. "But no matter how much confidence I have in you, I still feel responsible for them." She glanced up the stairway. Ki had appeared on the landing, carrying their saddlebags. Jessie frowned again, for she was once more aware of some subtle change in his appearance. She brushed aside her puzzlement and went on, "We'll be on our way, then. Look for us back tomorrow, late afternoon or early evening. It'll depend on how long we have to wait for the assay to be finished."

"Take your time and don't worry," O'Neill replied. "Your friends and I will be right here waiting for you."

"Our horses are waiting in the little stableyard behind the hotel," Ki said. "I managed to find a canteen to take with us, so we won't suffer if there's no water along the road."

"You won't suffer," O'Neill put in. "There's a little rill that runs close to the road most of the way. Now I'd better get upstairs and see what your friends plan to do today. We'll all be waiting right as rain when you two get back."

Jessie and Ki walked the few steps to the corner and turned into the street leading to the hotel's stable. Jessie glanced at Ki out of the corner of her eyes, still trying to resolve the puzzle that had perplexed her earlier. There was no obvious change in Ki's appearance, yet there was something about him that bothered her, a slight alteration she could not manage to understand.

As Ki had told her, the two saddled horses were waiting in the hotel's stableyard. He tossed Jessie's saddlebags over the rump of her mount and she stepped up to secure them with the saddle-strings while Ki attended to his own.

Riding side by side they went out the yawning gate,

reined their mounts into Gurley Street, and continued at a slow pace, the low-hanging sun in their faces. They'd gone only the short distance to Whiskey Row, and were passing the greenswarded grounds surrounding the Territorial Capitol, when an open buggy rolled out of the open space twenty yards or so ahead of them and wheeled into the street.

Against the sun-bright morning sky, the man in the buggy was visible to them only as a black silhouette. He looked back at Jessie and Ki, then rose to his feet in the moving buggy. His arm rose and fell. Ki and Jessie saw the flashing arc of the *shuriken* only as a glittering silver arc in the blue sky, but Ki caught its significance at his first glimpse. Sliding his foot from the stirrup, he kicked Jessie's horse in its belly. The kick landed with a jolt hard enough to send the animal shying to one side.

As the horse snorted and danced away, Jessie turned in her saddle to look at Ki. She saw the glitter of the *shuriken* thrown by the man in the buggy as it neared Ki's bare head. She was drawing her Colt when Ki rose in the saddle, one of his own *shuriken* in his hand.

By this time the man in the buggy had thrown a second blade, its silvery points glistening as it flew toward Ki. The first *shuriken* struck Ki's head. It landed with the small, high-pitched scrape of steel meeting steel.

Ki was taking another throwing-blade from his pocket when the second *shuriken* thrown by the man in the buggy hit the base of his neck. It shied off with another high-pitched rasping of steel on steel.

Ki flinched, but tossed his second blade. The man in the buggy was now clawing at his throat. Ki's *shuriken* cut into his attacker's pawing hands, bringing a spurt of blood. As Ki moved, Jessie's jaw dropped when she saw his black hair falling in thick bunches from his head. She tore her eyes away long enough to glance ahead.

Their assailant was crumpling over the back of the buggy-seat now, his life pouring from him in pulsing red gouts of bright arterial blood that spattered on the graveled street. Ki was spurring his horse ahead, a fresh *shuriken* already in his hand. When he saw his assailant sag and hang limply across the back of the buggy-seat, he tucked the *shuriken* back into his vest pocket.

"Ki!" Jessie exclaimed as she reached him. She saw his coal-black hair falling in disheveled strands from a bright gash in his head where his attacker's *shuriken* had landed. "Are you all right?"

"Of course," Ki replied. His voice was as composed as it always was during their casual conversations. "But I'm afraid we're going to have some explaining to do." He looked at the imposing facade of the Territorial Capitol, where the doors were now yawning wide and men were running from them toward the buggy. Then he added, "But I'm sure that between you and Bucky O'Neill, we'll be able to satisfy the authorities."

★

Chapter 15

"Don't you think it's time you told me what you've been up to?" Jessie asked as she stared in amazement at Ki.

There was a long, thick strand of tangled glistening black hair—obviously not Ki's own—hanging over one of his shoulders, and a dull black bare spot showed on his head. The white scarf around his neck was slashed on one side into ravels of thread.

"I'll tell you quickly, before those men from the capital get here," he replied. "That dead man in the buggy is the *kobu-do* Chijin warned me about last night."

"We'll never know who hired him to kill you, then." Jessie frowned. "Even if we're sure it was Manfield, we wouldn't be able to prove it."

"That does not matter. He will not harm anybody again," Ki replied. "But last night, when I realized he'd almost certainly make his attack with *shuriken,* it occurred to me that armor was the only way I could protect my head

172

and throat. You know yourself, Jessie, that a *shuriken* has to hit the skull or jugular vein to be immediately fatal."

"I should know." Jessie smiled. "You repeated it enough when you were trying to teach me to throw *shuriken*."

"So I went out last night looking for a blacksmith who could make a piece of armor that would protect my head and throat without being visible."

"But where on earth"— Jessie indicated the long strands of hair hanging from Ki's head and shoulders—"Where did you find somebody in a town like this?"

"I'll tell you later," Ki replied, gesturing toward the men approaching them. "We're going to have some explaining to do, and you're much better at that than I am. After we soothe those men down and start to the mine again, I'll tell you the whole story. Luck had a lot more to do with it than skill, but the main thing is that my unlikely idea worked out."

Almost two hours passed before Ki had the opportunity to satisfy Jessie's curiosity. During those two hours of questioning in the chambers of Arizona Territory's attorney general, the frame of one door in that gentleman's office was scarred and splintered by the repeated demonstrations which Ki gave to prove the accuracy and effectiveness of a *shuriken* thrown by someone who was skilled in the martial arts of the Orient.

At last, after the attorney general gave the opinion that Ki acted in self-defense, and that no charges were to be made against him, he and Jessie were allowed to continue their interrupted trip. The sun was heading for its zenith when they took the road again, and as their horses moved at a steady, mile-eating gait over the baked yellowish earth of the trail, Jessie turned to Ki.

"Why in the world didn't you tell me what you'd been

doing last night?" she asked. "You know I'd have understood."

"I never doubted that you would have, Jessie," Ki assured her. "But if I'd told you, you'd have been watching the road and anybody on it so openly that the *Kubo-do* in the buggy would have realized something was wrong. Then he'd have waited to make his attack, and all the work Joab Peters and I did last night might have been wasted."

"Perhaps I would have," she admitted. "Because from the time you came into the hotel dining-room this morning, I kept looking at you and wondering why you looked— well, just a little bit different. Joab did a remarkable bit of metalworking last night, to make that armor-plate contraption you were wearing on your head."

"He did, at that," Ki agreed. "I just asked him to make me a sort of metal skullcap that I could wear, and a collar. I knew the *Kubo-do* would aim for my head or my jugular vein; those are the targets anybody who understands the *shuriken* chooses. But it was Joab's idea to make a complete headpiece and bring it down to protect my throat and shoulders."

"And the headpiece fitted you almost like your own skin," Jessie said, shaking her head in fresh amazement. "But where did you find the long, black hair? It looked enough like your own to fool even me."

"There's a black horse in the Burke Hotel's stable that's going to have to grow a fresh crop of hair on its tail." Ki smiled. "It was Joab's idea, to cover that thin steel sheeting by gluing the hair on it to look like mine."

"It was a stroke of genius," Jessie said. "I kept staring at you, wondering why you looked just a little bit different, but I never did come up with the right answer."

"I suppose I could've shaved my head and used my own hair." Ki frowned. "But Joab knew exactly what to do.

174

He's made—well, maybe hundreds of unusual metal objects, like the copper figureheads that he crafted for Alex's first ships, back in San Francisco. Running into him here was just one of those strange coincidences that happen only once in a lifetime."

"It certainly saved your life," Jessie agreed. She shook her head and went on, "Now, if we can just get to the Iron King and back, and the assay results show that there's a good lode in that new mine Manfield started, this trip will certainly have been worthwhile."

As the sun peaked and started to descend toward the low crests of the Weaver Mountains, Jessie and Ki kept up their steady pace. They stopped only once, to eat the sandwiches provided by the hotel's kitchen, but sunset was beginning to gild the mountaintops before they saw the high round chimney of the Iron King's smelter rising in the distance. The breeze that almost always begins with the promise of nightfall was stirring the low bushes that were scattered over the yellow soil flanking the trail, and after their long hot ride both Jessie and Ki breathed the cool air gratefully.

"It looks like we'll make it to the mine before full dark," Jessie said, nodding toward the chimney. "And I'll be very glad to stop, but I'm about equally anxious to start back. I wonder if the assayer works at night."

"Even if he doesn't, we can ask him to do us a favor and run tests on the ore samples in your saddlebag," Ki pointed out.

"Yes, of course. I'd be glad to pay him for putting in the extra time," Jessie said.

They rode on through the deepening sunset, and before night had shrouded the landscape completely, reached the yellow brick office buildings and bunkhouse and the big shed that housed the hoist. Nestled close by was a smaller building, and as they reined in a man came out of it. He looked at what to him must have been an oddly assorted pair, then walked up to the hitchrail where they were tethering their horses.

"Evening, folks," he said. "I saw you pulling up, and when I spotted you for strangers, I figured I'd better come over and tell you that if you're looking for a place to stop for the night, you'll need to push on about four miles."

"But our business is here, with the Iron King's assayer," Jessie told him.

"Oh, now that's different. We've got a guest house for folks who visit the mine on business. And if you're looking for the assayer, that's me. Bud Snider's my name."

"I'm Jessie Starbuck, Mr. Snider. This is Ki. I understand that the Empire mine up in Prescott has its assay work done here," Jessie went on.

"Yes, indeed. Mr. Manfield, that'd be. Do you work for him, Miss—" Snider stopped and stared at Jessie, then asked, "Did I hear your name right? You did say Starbuck, didn't you?"

Jessie nodded. "I certainly did."

"Well, that's sure a name I recognize," Snider said, smiling. "I don't think there's anybody connected with mining who doesn't. First your father, and then you, have been written up in just about every mining journal in the world." He hesitated, then went on, "I hope you won't mind if I ask you a question?"

"Certainly not. Go ahead," Jessie replied.

"Does you being here mean that the Empire is going to be taken over by the Starbuck interests?"

"Not at all," Jessie replied. "I'm here with an old and very dear friend from the East, who owns a large block of stock in the Empire. Since you've been assaying their ore, I'm sure you know what's happened there."

"Yes, and I'm sorry to see it happen," Snider said. "The lode seems to be just about played out."

"Well, acting on behalf of my friend, I've brought some samples from a new vein that's just been opened. Naturally, she wants to know how it will prove out on an assay."

"Of course." Snider nodded. "And since you're acting on behalf of a stockholder, I'll be glad to run the samples the first thing in the morning. Of course, you'll have the use of our guest house tonight, and meals at our mess hall."

"Then that solves our problem of a place to stay tonight," Jessie replied. "But I wonder if I could impose on you?"

"In what way?"

"Ki and I are very anxious to get back to Prescott as soon as possible. Could you perhaps run your tests this evening?"

Snider hesitated only for a moment before nodding. "I'll be glad to oblige you, Miss Starbuck. Now, let me show you and your friend to the guest house, and point out the mess hall. Then I'll meet you here at the office after supper and run the tests."

"I suppose you're familiar with the assay process, Miss Starbuck?" Bob Snider asked as he gestured toward the doors of the three small ovens that broke the brick facing of the furnace, which filled one side of the assay office. A long, marble-topped workbench stood at right angles to the furnaces. Small porcelain bowls, a large bronze mortar and pestle, several brown bottles filled with liquids, a line of metal cans, and a large balance-scale stood on the bench.

"No, not the technical details," Jessie replied. "That's something I've never had time to study."

"Well, it's not at all complicated. I'll put a few ounces

177

of each one of your ore samples through a screen that separates the pieces of ore from the loose dirt," Snider went on.

As he spoke, the assayer was spooning dirt from one of the leather bags into a small, fine-meshed sieve. He shook the sieve over a bucket until only a dozen or so pebbles rattled around on its mesh bottom. Then he emptied the pebbles into a bronze mortar and reduced them to a coarse dust with its pestle.

Moving with the careful skill that bespoke long experience, Snider measured out a small heap of the powder with the scale and emptied it into one of the bowls, measured a similar quantity of black powder from one of the bottles, and sprinkled it over the crushed ore. Reaching into one of the cans, he brought up a quantity of shotgun pellets in his cupped palm and dribbled them into the cup.

"Powdered charcoal and lead pellets," he explained. "The charcoal oxidizes even the tiniest flakes of gold or silver ore that're mixed with the rock, and the ore fuses with the lead. When it cools, we'll have what's called the *dorè* button in the bottom of this dish."

"But how do you separate the gold and silver from the charcoal and lead?" Ki asked.

"By pouring nitric acid over the button after it cools, to dissolve the lead and silver," Snider replied. "Then, when I weigh the gold, it's a simple job of multiplication to tell how much pure gold there is in a ton of raw ore."

"And that will tell us whether it'll be profitable to work the new vein," Jessie mused.

"And you'll get an even better idea after I precipitate the silver from the acid," Snider said. "But it'll take quite a bit of time for me to run all these samples you've brought. You're welcome to stay and watch, if you like, but you won't get a lot of sleep. And if you're starting back to Prescott tomorrow—"

178

While the assayer was talking, Jessie and Ki exchanged glances and nods. Jessie broke in on Snider to say, "We'll stay here, Mr. Snider. I'm sure neither Ki nor I will sleep very soundly until we know what you've found out. Go ahead and make your tests."

"I'll really be happy to bring Lucy some good news for a change," Jessie told Ki as they neared the first houses on the outskirts of Prescott. "After looking at the assay reports, I'd say the new vein Manfield tried to open secretly is going to be even richer than the one that petered out."

"What about Manfield?" Ki asked. "He certainly can't be left in charge of the Empire after what he's done."

"Of course not. But the law will take care of him. The first thing we'll do when we get to the hotel will be to get Lucy a lawyer to represent her. I'm sure Mr. Cassidy will know who to recommend."

"It should be an open and shut case," Ki commented. "But we'll have to stay here to testify, won't we?"

"Perhaps we can persuade the attorney general to speed things up," Jessie replied, nodding toward the Territorial Capitol building just ahead. "Especially after that demonstration of the *shuriken* you gave him."

"It'll be worth a try," Ki agreed.

"Oh, I think we'll succeed, Ki," Jessie said. "It's not too late in the day; he may still be in his office. Let's stop and find out."

After hearing Jessie's story the attorney general hemmed and hawed for a moment. Then he said, "I think you can safely leave Mr. Manfield to be dealt with by a criminal grand jury, Miss Starbuck. I'll start the process of empaneling one at once."

"But that will take time, too." Jessie frowned. "And all of us will have to stay here to testify."

179

"Not necessarily. As much as we'd like for you and your friends to stay for a while in our territory, I'll send one of my staff members to the hotel tomorrow morning to take your depositions."

"What about Manfield?" Jessie asked.

"He'll be arrested as soon as your depositions are in my hands. That's all we'll need; the grand jury will do the rest, and my office staff will introduce your depositions and testify to their validity."

Jessie and Ki rode on into town, reined their horses into the Burke Hotel's stableyard, and dismounted. Ki threw their saddlebags over his shoulder, and they started for the hotel. They were passing through the lobby when they saw Bucky O'Neill coming down the stairs.

"Bucky!" Jessie smiled. "Where are Lucy and Steve?"

"They're both upstairs in Mrs. Chalmers's room," O'Neill said. "I just came down to get them a pot of tea from the restaurant."

"Go ahead and get it, then, but make it a big pot," Jessie told him. "Ki and I brought back some very good news for her and Steve, and since you've been so much a part of our group, you should hear it, too."

After Jessie told Lucy and Steve the results of their trip, Lucy sighed with relief. "Thank goodness! Now Steve and I can finish our trip without any worry." Turning to Steve, she went on, "We'll take the train tomorrow, and spend the rest of the time on our tour seeing a lot more of this beautiful country."

Steve and Jessie had been exchanging covert glances while Lucy talked, and Jessie answered the question in his eyes with an almost indiscernible nod.

"What about you, Bucky?" Jessie asked O'Neill. "The stockholders in the Empire Mine are going to have to hire a

180

new manager, and I'm sure Lucy would support you if you applied for the job."

"Well, I thank you kindly, Jessie," O'Neill answered, shaking his head. "But I don't know all that much about mining, or business, either. Anyhow, I've got my mind set on the job I want before too long. The sheriff here's getting old, and I figure I'll run for the job in the next election."

"Then I wish you luck," Jessie told him. "And I'm sure all the rest of us do." Looking around the room, but with a special message in her eyes for Steve, she went on, "And I think I'm going to let our tea be my supper. It's been a long day, and I intend to get to bed as fast as I can."

In the dim light of the new dawn, Jessie stirred, and a soft sigh escaped her lips as the sensation of Steve's lips caressing her breasts roused her from sleep.

"Again?" she whispered before Steve's lips covered hers.

"Yes. And then again," he replied. "I don't want our last day together to be a short one."

By this time Steve was pressing his body to Jessie's, and she could feel his erection throbbing against her thighs. She opened herself then to his lusty penetration, and held him to her still-quivering form after they'd reached the heights. Then Jessie brought into play the subtle contracting caresses taught her by the wise old geisha, and again and yet again they repeated their flights of passion until the sun was spilling through the window.

"Now that our problems—or Lucy's problems—are all settled, Ki, I'll be as glad to get on the train and head back to Texas as she and Steve were to finish their trip," Jessie remarked as Ki gathered up their bags the next morning.

"Yes. We've had enough to do here," Ki said as they

started down the stairs. They went down the last few steps and were passing the reception desk when Manfield stepped from behind one of the tall pillars that graced the lobby.

"I've had all of your interference with my affairs that I can stand, Jessica Starbuck!" he shouted. His eyes were glaring wildly and his face livid with rage. "Now you're going to pay for the meddling you've done!"

Manfield's right hand was hidden in the folds of his long coat. He raised it now, the little nickleplated Whitney pocket pistol he held gleaming in the subdued light of the big lobby.

Ki had dropped the luggage and reached for his *shuriken* the minute he saw the mine manager's arm start up. As Manfield swung the gun to aim at Jessie, the *shuriken* left Ki's hand and sailed in a glittering arc that ended when the throwing-blade sliced through Manfield's collar and into his jugular vein.

Manfield fired, but his arm flinched when he saw the gleam of Ki's weapon. The slug intended for Jessie went wide, and raised only a puff of dust from the high back of the chair beside her. The sharp bite of the *shuriken* drove all thoughts of a second shot from Manfield's mind. He dropped the gun to claw at Ki's blade, and he succeeded in dislodging it. Then the gout of arterial blood that gushed from his throat took its toll, and he sagged to the floor.

"Are you all right, Jessie?" Ki asked.

"Yes." Jessie nodded. She'd drawn her Colt an instant too late to beat Ki's blade with a shot, and she holstered the weapon with a relieved exhalation as she looked at Manfield's huddled, motionless form. Gesturing at the mine manager's prone body, she added, "And he'd still be alive if he'd been honest."

"Miss Starbuck!" a man gasped as he rushed to join the

182

small group that was forming around Manfield's body. "I'm glad your man was so quick to act! I saw him demonstrate those little blades the other day in the attorney general's office, but I really didn't think they were so deadly."

As Jessie stared at the man, frowning as she tried to place him, he saw her puzzlement and went on, "I'm Schroeder, the attorney general's assistant. "I was coming here to get you to sign some papers, and I saw the whole incident."

"You won't need the papers now that Manfield's dead," Jessie said thoughtfully. "But Ki and I have a train to catch, and if you'd take care of this matter for us, we won't have to delay another day in starting home."

"Of course!" Schroeder nodded. "I'll be glad to."

Jessie turned to Ki and went on, "We'll make our train after all. And I'll be glad to be home where it's a bit more peaceful."

"So will I," Ki agreed. Then he smiled and added, "It looks like we'll get back to the Circle Star in time to relax and rest before we have to start the gathers."

Watch for

LONE STAR AND THE COMANCHEROS

sixty-ninth novel in the exciting
LONE STAR
series from Jove

coming in May!